About the Author

Lily lives in Hampshire with her husband and children and two laid-back, if somewhat lazy, dogs called Benji and Jet. When she isn't writing, you can guarantee she'll be walking along the beach for new plot lines and twists. Or in the water, paddle boarding. She has a passion for all things Harry Potter and is a proud Ravenclaw as well as a love of the Marvel movies and Rom-Coms. You can follow Lily on Twitter @LilyDGioAuthor and on Instagram: -Lily Di Giovanni also on her Facebook author page.

Time for a Fresh Start

To Linda,
Best Wishes, lovely

Lily & Giovanni
xx

Lily Di Giovanni

Time for a Fresh Start

Olympia Publishers
London

www.olympiapublishers.com
OLYMPIA PAPERBACK EDITION

A CIP catalogue record for this title is
available from the British Library.

ISBN: 978-1-80074-079-2

This is a work of fiction.
Names, characters, places and incidents originate from the writer's
imagination. Any resemblance to actual persons, living or dead, is
purely coincidental.

First Published in 2022

Olympia Publishers
Tallis House
2 Tallis Street
London
EC4Y 0AB

Printed in Great Britain

Dedication

To Richard and Helen Piper, my grandfather and
grandmother,
for starting my journey and building up that passion within
me for the love of literature and reading.

Acknowledgements

Firstly, I need to say once again a huge thank you to my publishing team at Olympia Publishers, from the editor James Houghton for taking another chance on me. Next, to Kristina Smith from the production side of things and all her hard work. The graphics team and the proofreaders, thank you all for bringing this book together. It's a huge team effort and I couldn't ask for a better team to work alongside. I couldn't possibly forget Fiona from the publicity side, many thanks for the kind words and keeping me calm all the times we've talked. I know that with the current situations we have had to face the past year has been difficult for everyone, however without our publishers, we authors couldn't possibly continue with our books and sales that you provide. So thank you each and every one of you.

A huge amount of gratitude has to go once again to my husband and children, for putting up with me talking about characters and plot lines as well as getting their individual advice of how something might play out. Also, to my good friend, Sharon who has helped in regard to ideas on how to follow through with titles, as this is going to be a series of books.

Lastly and most importantly you the reader, it is overwhelming and a dream come true that I am able to bring my stories to life. Thank you for taking the time to buy and read my books, it truly means the world to me and may I be able to bring you many more.

CHAPTER ONE

I just cannot seem to shift this uneasy feeling in the pit of my stomach. These awful thoughts swimming around in my head, that are refusing to disappear, as they haunt me on my way home from working the night shift.

It isn't work that is making me feel weird, actually work is going really well. I work at my local hospital, St Vincent's, as a nurse on the emergency admissions ward or for short EAU. It can be so full on at times and extremely stressful but I wouldn't change my job for the world. I've been working as a nurse now for around four years and it's the best job move, I ever made, well it was at the time. Wow, has it really been four years, boy where has the time gone? Each shift I do is always different from the previous one you did before, you never get two shifts the same and you never get a shift that is quiet.

Night shifts are ideal for me as it fits my home life perfectly. Recently though something hasn't sat right with me at home and I just can't put my finger on the problem. Oh, I don't know it could just be me and my paranoia, over thinking and seeing things that aren't there. All I can say is that Jason has been acting a little suspiciously recently. Well, no, that isn't quite the truth, something isn't setting right since Jason's mobile statement came through the post. I cannot wait to see my closest friend Millie on Friday, it can't come soon enough. We are meeting up to have some lunch and a drink or two and blow off some steam. Millie is so good to talk to and I like to get her viewpoint on things and see what she thinks, it'll be good to get some outside prospective on the situation. Put it this way, if Millie thinks I'm being stupid or paranoid, she will let me know, she isn't scared to speak her mind, trust me. So for now I need to let this go until I see her.

"Bloody hell, it's cold out there Millie. It is so deceiving, such a beautiful sunny day but that wind is so icy. Oh, great, you've already got me a glass of wine waiting, spot on." As I take my first gulp of the tangy dry white wine, I enjoy the taste sensation as it goes down my throat.

"So, Amber, how's your week been? You sounded upset and distant the other day on the phone, everything okay with you and Jason?"

This is the reason why I love Millie. I've only been here — what? — no longer than five minutes and she is straight to the point. I think she knows me better then I know myself, the only problem is I feel really silly for doubting my relationship now and I just want to enjoy my girly day without getting upset, and maybe start to worry over nothing.

"Oh, it's probably nothing, just me being silly as you know how I can get. I would rather leave it and just enjoy today, it's been a while. How's work going anyway?"

"Good, busy the usual really and don't try to change the subject Amber, don't think I don't notice that you do that. It's okay though, after a couple more drinks I would have loosened that tongue of yours."

Shit, I think to myself, I'd better take my time and maybe

get something to eat. Drinking wine on an empty stomach and being suspicious that my boyfriend is cheating on me isn't a good combination. Loose lips sink ships and all that. No, I must take my time and pace myself.

A couple of hours later after a lovely chicken club sandwich and starting on my third glass of wine, those negative thoughts about Jason are increasing, Millie is telling me something but I'm not taking it in. What if Jason is cheating and I'm not being paranoid, what would I do then? Could I be able to forgive him and move forward? Would I scream and shout and let him have it? Would my life as I know it be over, shit what would I do?

"You haven't heard a word I've said, have you Amber?"

"Shit, I'm so sorry Millie I didn't mean to be rude, I was in my own little world there for a moment, again I'm sorry, what were you saying?"

"No, it's all right, don't worry about it. It is obvious that you have something more important on your mind. Do you want to share it? As you know, I am a good listener. Knowing you as I do, if you don't share it, it will only eat away at you. Now come on tell Auntie Millie all about it and if I can give you advice I will, if I think you are over thinking things I'll tell you. As they say, a problem shared is a problem solved, or is it halved or whatever? Come on, spill, I know you want to."

She is right, I do need to talk about it, as I don't want anyone to take me for a fool and treat me like I'm a mug, laughing behind my back whilst they continue to humiliate me. I need that second opinion.

"Should we settle up here and get a taxi back to mine? You can ring Jason and tell him you won't be back tonight as you are sleeping over at my place, okay? We'll stop off at the shop and get a bottle of wine and some cigs. Once back at mine you can tell me what's wrong okay."

"Okay, sounds like a plan," I say to her.

Grateful that she can read my mind, knowing exactly what I need, when I need it. Once we have paid the bill, as well as leave a small tip and get outside the bar I'm surprised to find it's dark. Heck, how long have we been in there for? I get my phone out to ring Jason and I notice the time, wow it's just gone six! Have we really been in there for four hours? Where the hell has the time gone? As I'm about to press the call button on my phone, a burst of anger comes over me. I ignore the call button and instead I swipe over to my message icon and quickly type out a message to Jason to let him know I'm going to be staying over at Millie's tonight and press send.

"I couldn't be arsed to ring him, I just sent him a quick text," I say to Millie.

"Good girl, now come on I'm flipping freezing," Millie laughs back at me, as we link arms and walk through the town to the taxi rank.

Once we get back to Millie's she gets me some slops to get changed into, so I can feel more comfortable and relaxed as we chill, talk and drink some more. Back downstairs she has put the television on quietly with her favourite music channel playing, so we have some kind of background noise. As she pours us both a glass of wine, she looks over at me.

"Right are you going to spill the beans, or what? Come on I've known you long enough and can read you like a book. So out with it, what has the jackass done now?"

"Don't be like that, Millie, and honestly, it's probably just me being oversensitive and overthinking things. Oh, shit,

Millie, the only thing is though, I don't actually think I am this time. Something has happened and his explanations just don't add up, it simply doesn't make any sense, that's all," I say back to her.

"Well, you know what they say, a problem shared and all that, as I said earlier to you," Millie says in response.

Oh well, what's the worst that can happen? Well, apart from me making a fool of myself and coming across as insecure and stupid or even worse looking for something that isn't there, because let's face it, when everything starts going really good in your life, you start to look for the problems and the negatives because life is never that straightforward and perfect.

"Well, you know I've been working a lot of over time the last couple of months since Jason lost his job. Well, last month I started to notice changes in his behaviour."

"What kind of changes? He may just be down due to the fact of losing his job and he may feel a bit worthless as you are now the sole earner. Men generally don't like that, they like to see themselves as the head of the household, bringing home the bacon and all that, and when the roles change unexpectedly then that could have an impact on his male ego," Millie tries to reason.

"No Millie it isn't anything like that, he's become distant and kind of secretive. We haven't had sex for the past two and a half months, he never wants to touch me, not even a hug. He is always moody and when I try and get him to talk, he practically bites my head off. I mean what's all that about? Then there is his phone. He will never leave it lying around like he used to do, it's always in his hand or pocket. When it rings or he gets a text he goes straight into another room and then there's the phone bill at the end of last month." I start to cry because as I am saying these words out loud for the first time, I know I should be worried. The signs are there, clear as the nose on my face, Millie interrupts my thought process.

"What do you mean about the phone bill last month? What is the relevance of a bloody phone bill?"

I laugh out loud because if I don't, I will only cry even more and I refuse to weep. "His mobile phone statement was nearly five hundred pounds and no matter how many times I ask him what the hell has he been using his phone for, he hasn't got an explanation and just keeps saying that the phone company have made a mistake. When I tell him to ring up the mobile network he's with, and question it, he refuses to do it. He is up to something, isn't he?" I cry to Millie even though I told myself I wouldn't, that Jason wasn't worth one of my tears.

It wasn't to be though as the tears just kept coming, it was as though a dam had burst its banks. All the feelings and built-up emotions I had kept hidden, were finally coming to the surface, in large angry drops of water and my eyes were the taps that had been turned on to full blast. Poor Millie, her top was getting soaked and it didn't help that my mascara was running down my face and dropping onto her T-shirt. What a mess I must look, a very bad ugly version of Alice Cooper that had gone through a car wash. Once the tears had subsided and I was finally managing to calm down I pushed myself away from Millie and I looked at her, hoping she wouldn't see me as pathetic and a hopeless case who needed to have a good shake. I needn't have worried because the next thing that came out of her mouth was, "You need to get the bastard's phone, we need to think of a way for you to get your hands on that damn phone and see what evidence you can find on it. Until you do that, you need to act as though nothing is wrong, go about your days as you do now. Then one morning when you come home from one off your night shifts, creep quietly into your bedroom without waking him and grab hold of his mobile. It may be your only opportunity especially if he takes it everywhere with him. It's the only thing I can think of. Unless, well you could wait until he has a shower. Would that work?" Millie asks me.

"No, that wouldn't work at all, as he takes it into the bathroom with him because he likes to listen to his music," I tell Millie in reply to her question. In response to Millie's first idea, after pondering over it I simply tell her, "You know something? I think your first idea makes a lot more sense and he wouldn't expect it either as I always shower when I get in from work then get some sleep, as I am always too tired to do anything else after finishing a shift."

Millie comes over to me and gives me a kiss and a huge hug and simply says, "Be strong, I'm here for you. Right, now we have that out of the way, let's enjoy the rest of the evening. Should we order a pizza, because, I don't know about you but I'm pretty hungry now."

I wake up the following morning feeling worse for wear. The actual sunlight is hurting my eyes and I think a couple of drummers have moved into my head, as the drumming sounds and banging is so overwhelming that I need some painkillers and definitely in need of coffee. I'm trying to recall how much alcohol did we manage to put away last night, I didn't think it was that much but my head this morning is saying something totally different. Once I have had some aspirin and a couple cups of coffee, I go and wash my face and sort myself out. Millie is still dead to the world, so I quietly slip out and leave her a note thanking her for a great night and her advice and that I will ring her, later.

Thank goodness it is a lovely sunny Saturday morning outside. You can actually feel the heat of the sun today and no hint of any cold wind, it was just what the doctor ordered whilst I clear my mind on my long walk home. I am so grateful that I don't have a shift tonight, I think that I will be ordering some Chinese food, and watching a movie this evening' I'll see if Jason wants to do the same thing, it might be good for us to do something together. I love the walk home especially when it's a day like today. The snowdrops and daffodils have all fully bloomed and you can make out all the new buds on the trees. Then you have all the different songs and music coming from all the different species of birds it has to be one of my favourite sounds, especially when it comes to the cooing of the wood pigeons, I could listen to them all day long as it brings me a sense of peace.

As I continue on my walk home, I ponder over the plan and what Millie said last night. Do I actually have the balls and the confidence to sneak Jason's phone away from him whilst he's asleep? What if he wakes up and catches me in the act, what will I say? What if the nerves get the better of me? No, I cannot think negative thoughts, I will have to find the guts from somewhere within, no pun intended because I simply cannot carry on like this and waste any more of my time, energy and life on a relationship that isn't going anywhere. So with my mind made up I will have to be patient and wait for the perfect opportunity to catch the cheating bastard. Weird, isn't it? How I have already condemned the bloke for cheating, without any proof but I just know, call it women's intuition. When a woman gets that gut feeling, then nine out of ten times she is absolutely right.

As I walk through the front door, I am starting to feel more human again, the walk did me the world of good. As I walk towards the kitchen the smell of bacon tingles my senses and my mouth starts watering, which then sets of my stomach. I am starving.

"Hi there, any chance of making me one?" I ask Jason.

"No, this is the last of it and before you ask, no you can't have a bite, you can go out to the corner shop and buy some if you want one."

"Wow, that's rude don't you think? Bloody hell Jason, all I've done is come through the door and already you have an attitude towards me. I'll tell you what, why don't I just leave you to it, I'm going for a shower if that's all right with you." You fricking pillock, I think to myself. As I get undressed and get into the shower the tears come out of nowhere. I let the luscious hot water coming from the showerhead wash away the tears. The water feels wonderful on my skin. I just stand there enjoying the sensuous heat coming from the water as it hits me in the face and splashes over my body. Once I have washed my hair and soaped the rest of my body I turn and let the water hit my back, letting it give me a gentle massage. Just before I am ready to turn the shower off, Jason bursts into the bathroom making me scream out loud.

"Crikey Jason, what's up? Is everything okay?"

"What do you mean?"

"Well, you've come bursting into the bathroom like a bat out of hell, as though something is terribly wrong."

"Oh right, well no everything is good, I've just come to get some of my shit together. I'm going away for the rest of the weekend with the lads."

"What, wait hold on a minute, when did this come about?" I say as I scrabble out of the shower and quickly grab a towel. Wrapping it around my body, I follow Jason downstairs still soaking wet from the shower.

"I thought I told you, it has been planned for a while."

"No, Jason, you never told me and you know you didn't."

How can he just drop this on me? I am doing my best to control the sudden angry emotions that are currently starting to overwhelm me. I know for a fact that he never once mentioned it.

"Well, what does it matter anyway? You stayed out last night, so now it's my turn."

"So what? This is tit for tat, is that it? I was hoping for us to spend the evening together, get take-out and watch a movie. Can you actually afford to go out, or will it be me funding it once again?" I shout angrily back at him.

"You can be a right bitch, do you know that, Amber?"

With that said he storms off back into the kitchen.

"Piss off Jason, go on just do one, will you? You are a selfish bastard, what about spending time or an evening in with me, what about us? You are always out and last night was the first time in a couple of months for me as I am always working to cover us."

I am so angry and frustrated and I know I shouldn't have said that about the money, I just wanted to press his buttons because he was playing tit for tat all because I'd stayed out last night. No there is much, much more to this, than meets the eye. From out of nowhere though I started to think to myself, is Jason acting like this on purpose because he wants out but he doesn't want to look like the bad guy by being the one to call time on us? Would he really push me so far where I can't put up with his bullshit any more, so then I am the one to finish the relationship by breaking up with him? As I go back upstairs to get dressed and think about what's going on in my head, I hear the front door slam shut and out of pettiness I shout out at the top of my voice, "No need to slam doors you prick!" At that moment with the way I feel it wouldn't hurt if we finished things, it would be a relief if truth be told, but that is because I am so angry with him.

Come six o'clock I'm on the phone ordering my usual Chinese food, chicken and sweetcorn soup, large crispy pancake roll and pork chow mein. I think I will wash it down with a bottle of coke. As I'm chilling on the sofa going through the TV channels, seeing what Saturday night television has to offer, my phone starts to ring. As I look at the screen, I notice it's work. Oh, flipping heck, shit, shit, shit, I think to myself, this is the last thing I really need right now, especially when I'm supporting a post hangover from last night. Should I ignore the call and let it go straight to voicemail or should I just bite the bullet and get the call over with? Without thinking too much about it, I grab my phone and answer the call.

"Hello," I say.

"Hi, Amber, it's Gina, listen I know it's your weekend off, but is there any way you can come in this evening, or tomorrow night, sorry to ask, but Catherine has rung in sick."

"I can't tonight Gina, sorry but I'm not fit for wear but you can put my name down to do Catherine's shift tomorrow night, I just need a good night's sleep."

"Cheers, Amber, you're a star. I will see you tomorrow night."

With that we say our goodbyes and I go back to waiting for my takeaway and watching Saturday night TV actually feeling lonely and sad. I don't even bother to get in touch with Jason. I send a quick message to Millie telling her I'm now working tomorrow evening and I'll have a gossip with her, then.

As Sunday night approaches I'm getting ready for work and still Jason isn't home, I haven't heard a word from him. So before I leave I write him a note:

Hi Jason,
Sorry babe, but I got called
into work. hope you had a
good time and I will see
you tomorrow at some
point.

Love Amber

As I arrive onto the ward to start my shift, it is so busy and you can see straight away how short staffed we are. I head into the ladies and switch my jumper for my blue work tunic and put plenty of deodorant on. If we get caught coming into work with full uniform then we could end up getting a right ticking off by the ward sister, more so if you get caught out after a shift has finished. Especially with cross contamination and all. Once I'm changed and have all my pens, fob watch and name badge, I head to the kitchen and get myself a coffee and make my way back to the ward office. The ward board is looking a bit hectic and we've had a complete turn-around of patients in the last forty-eight to seventy-two hours. I have a feeling there is going to be quite a few bed moves tonight onto other wards, to make new bed spaces for those coming to us from A&E. I go and print off the handovers from the computer for the rest of the staff that are coming in to start their shifts and wait on Gina to come and give me the hand over for my patients this evening. Looks like I'm going to be at the bottom half of the ward for my shift, which I don't mind, as that can be at times somewhat quieter than the top end. Once we've had our handover, I start going around my jobs and saying hello to my patients. I make sure my patients have had their OB's done and medication has been given out and signed for. Once the patients are settled for the night and room lights have been switched off, and the corridor lights dimmed, I make a call to switchboard and it's Millie who answers.

"Wow, just the person I was calling for, it's me Amber. Was seeing if you were in or not, do you fancy a coffee break in about an hour?"

"Hi hon, you got called in again I see."

"Haha, you know it, they know I cannot say no. Anyway, what about that coffee? I can come downstairs to your office if you like or you could come up here to the ward."

"Yes, you come down here as there is only me on switchboard tonight and I can't really leave unless I really need the toilet."

"Okay, no worries. Be down in about an hour or so."

CHAPTER TWO

As I hang up, a new patient arrives onto the ward from A&E. So I go to get the handover and I ask Katie, one of the healthcare assistants to do the MRSA swabs, OB's and to get the lady a fresh jug of water with ice and a glass. Once I have received handover, I go to my female patient Mary and fill in the necessary paperwork that all wards have to complete. The usual protocol real name, address, next of kin, any allergies etc etc. Once I've completed the paperwork, I go and lock Mary's medications into the top drawer of her bedside locker and the rest of her belongings into the lower cupboard of the same locker. I write Mary's name on the board that's on the wall above her bed, as well as the doctor who is in charge off Mary's care and will be looking after her. Once that is all done, I get Mary settled and dim down her lights, when a text comes through on my phone. I have a quick look at the screen I see that it is from Jason, so I nip quickly into the ladies to read his message:

> Just got back in,
> thanks for the note,
> no surprise though to
> be honest. Work comes
> first with you. I see you
> when I see you, I guess.

It's half past two in the morning and he's just getting back in now, it's a bloody joke that's what it is. It hasn't escaped my notice either that there are no kisses or love from Jason, that in itself is so upsetting and frustrates me. What did he expect me to do, sit at home on my own twiddling my thumbs and waiting until he got back in. Not only that, but put up with his drunken nonsense and crap that will no doubt spill out of his mouth. No way, not me. Of course I would choose to go to work. My job matters, I get to help others and be there for the sick and the injured, they need me. I am not going to feel bad about that and I'm certainly not going to apologise for anything either. I put my phone back in my pocket and go back to work. I'm not even going to warrant it with a response.

Come three o'clock I take my break and head downstairs to the switchboard office and have a coffee and a chat with Millie. Bless her, as I knock on the door for her to let me in, she looks all flustered and a bit stressed to say the least. As she lets me in, I say to her, "Tough night so far, I take it?"

"You're not joking, we definitely need more porters on a night. Why do so many patients need to go down to X-ray or for some form of scans through the night? There is no let-up and I haven't got enough porters on duty for the demands."

"Millie, take a deep breath, will you? You can only do your best. Oh, and the answer to your question, is the simple fact that the patients' needs change all the time depending on their circumstances, also it's what the doctors want which we have to follow, sorry."

"I know, I know. It's just stressful especially when you are on your own and getting the brunt of people's frustrations.

They too, need to understand that there is more than one ward that we have to cover in this damn hospital. I can't just magic up flipping porters with the click of my fingers. Right, let's get this coffee made, shall we, I need my caffeine fix."

I end up taking over and doing the coffees as her phone goes off another three times. Once she has managed to deal with whatever it is she has to do, we get a ten-minute breather.

"So how was your weekend, was Jason okay when you got back in?"

"My weekend was very quiet and lonely thanks. What about you, did you get up to much?"

"Nothing special really, spent a couple of hours down at the gym. Oh, I spoke to this really cool guy. He asked me out for a drink sometime and later on I went back home and did some household chores. Hold on a minute what do you mean lonely, was Jason not at home with you?"

"Well, he was when I got back first thing, then we had a terrible argument and he left slamming the front door and by the time I left for work tonight he still hadn't come home. Then about half two this morning I get a text saying that he had just got back and no surprise to find I had decided to put work first. So yeah, that about sums up my weekend. Oh, I did have a lovely Chinese takeaway, though."

"So let me get this right Amber, you haven't seen or heard from Jason since what time yesterday."

"Hmm, about eleven, or thereabouts I think."

"Where in the world has he been staying, then?"

"Well, the lads had planned a weekend away apparently and as I went out with you and stayed over Friday, then he had the right to do the same, even though I had no idea of these plans. Bloody hell is that the time? I need to get back upstairs Mil, I'm five minutes late. Listen wait for me outside the main entrance after work and I'll walk to the bottom of the road with you."

"Okay, no worries, hope the rest of your shift goes better than mine. See you later, Amber."

My shift goes by without too much trouble, the only thing that was time consuming was each new patient that arrived onto the ward from A&E. By the time we get the handover, have the OB's done on each individual, MRSA swabs and made sure their care files have been completed. Each patient took about thirty to forty-five minutes before they were checked onto the ward. Thank goodness we have nursing assistants to help us nurses out. By the time my shift has finished I am wiped out and exhausted. I haven't heard a word from Jason so he will no doubt be crashed out in bed, dead to the world (no pun intended). Once I have given the handover to the day staff, I go to the ladies to get changed out of my work uniform and into my normal day-to-day clothes and go to meet up with Millie.

I spot Millie waiting on the bench having a cigarette looking really tired. As she sees me coming out, she smiles at me and gets up and walks over in my direction.

"You didn't need to walk over to me as I was coming your way, you daft cow."

"What a bloody shift that was, so glad to be out of that shithole of an office."

"I take it, it didn't get any better then, when I left?"

"No, it wasn't that, I just had a few frustrated moments in

regard to the idiotic porters taking their damn time in view to their breaks, that's all. It really makes my blood boil as they know how short of staff we are and the number of jobs we had coming in from all the wards."

I try not to laugh out loud because when Millie is on one like this, she is so funny and she can carry it on for a while. So my way to try and calm her down is to change the subject the best way I can.

"Anyway, tell me about this cute guy from the gym, have you arranged to meet up with him yet or not?"

"Wow that wasn't subtle at all Amber," Millie says, as she laughs out herself. "Well, his name is Nate, and yes, he does go to the same gym as me. We have been talking a little here and there. Then one day he just said, 'Do you want to go out for a drink some time?' Then he gave me his number and that was that."

"So I guess he is leaving it up to you. In a way he has put the ball back in your court then, what are you going to do?"

"I think I will let him stew for a couple of days, you know me, I like to play hard to get. That's probably why I am still single to be honest," she says as she is still laughing.

Millie does worry me sometimes, I do wonder if she is really that happy to be on her own. She is a massive workaholic, when she isn't working then she is out partying and drinking just as hard as though her life depended on it. Millie is drop-dead gorgeous, and is never short of male attention. At five foot eight, extremely trim and toned and has that lovely Mediterranean tanned olive skin, long glossy locks and curves in the right places and an ample chest, she could have any guy she wanted. I just wished that she would find some nice fella that would make her want to settle down.

"Have you heard from Jason again?"

"No, I haven't heard a peep from him since his last text, to be honest he will no doubt be crashed out in bed, and because he's been drinking all weekend, he'll be out of it for a while to tell the truth."

"Well then if that is the case why don't you see if you can snatch his phone away from him? He wouldn't even notice. That way you could have a proper nosy and have it back next to him on his bedside cabinet and he would never even know that you had done anything."

"I couldn't intrude on his privacy like that, Mil. Come on, if someone did that to you or even me for that matter, you would be pissed off to say the least."

"All I'm saying, Amber, is if you want to know what Jason is being all suspicious about and plus the fact that he is doing whatever he can to hide his phone at all costs, this just might be the only opportunity to grab his damn phone and find out once and for all. At least it will put your mind at rest and Jason will never know. Well, that's unless you find something incriminating, then obviously you'll lose your shit."

"I think about it, I'll catch you later."

We say our goodbyes and give each other a hug and go our separate ways home.

CHAPTER THREE

As I walk home, I ponder on what Millie said and I do my best to recall Jason's behaviour over the last couple of months and I wonder, does it give me anything like a warrant or excuse to go through his phone? Then I switch it around in my head, what if Jason asked me for my phone would I let him have it? Well for one thing I have absolutely nothing to hide, so yes of course I would. However, when you switch it around again Jason would and does get so defensive and bolts out of the room. With that settled and my mind made up I enjoy the rest of my walk in the lovely, fresh, morning sunshine.

As I reach my front door, I very quietly open it and walk inside. There isn't a sound, all is still and silent. As I quietly close my door my phone makes a bleep sound indicating that a text has come through. I quickly get it out of my pocket, look at the screen and see it's from Millie. When I open her message, she is straight to the point:

> It will only take you a minute, Amber,
> if he is dead to the world, how will
> he know, and deep down, you know
> you want to. Stop being the sensible
> you and find out if he's cheating or
> not. DO IT, DO IT NOW.

I go into the kitchen to make myself an herbal tea and re-read Millie's message. She's right, of course she's right. Without thinking to much about it, I silently creep upstairs and make my way into the bedroom and to my shock I find that Jason isn't there. Thinking to myself that maybe he may have gone to bed in the spare bedroom so I wouldn't disturb him when I got in from work, so I go as quietly as possible along the landing (which only takes about five steps) to the spare room to check. As I open the door, I hear him snoring and there he is still fully dressed, out of it on the top of the bed. Shoes still on and the room stinks of a piss-up in a brewery. I briefly glance towards the bedside cabinet and discover that there isn't anything on it, but just as I am about to turn to leave the room, something on the floor catches my eye. Due to the way Jason is sprawled on the bed his right arm is hanging off the side, dangling, and there on the floor is his phone. He must have been on it before he fell into a deep drunken slumber and his mobile probably slipped from his hand. I go as quietly as possible further into the room, and as quickly as I can, I grab hold of the mobile and slip out of the room without disturbing him.

Once I am back downstairs, I pour some hot water into my cup with a lemon and ginger herbal tea bag and sit at the table just staring at Jason's phone. It's like it's getting enjoyment out of the fact that it is tormenting me, laughing at the fact that it is hiding all of Jason's secrets. All I wanna do is pick the damn thing up and throw it at the wall and watch it smash into little pieces. Instead, I unlock his mobile, I would have thought that the jackass would have at least changed his security code to get into it, but as I unlock it I see that there is a text from a number I don't even recognise and all I can do is stare at the message that simply says:

Good night babe, daddy to
be. Love you loads from
both me and the bump
xxx

I'm in shock and I don't know what to do, I leave the kitchen and go and lock myself into the downstairs bathroom just in case Jason decides to wake up and come down. I shakily retrieve my phone and send a quick text to Millie. Within the space of forty seconds my phone starts to vibrate.

"Hi Millie, I'm so sorry if you were sleeping, I didn't mean to wake you if that was the case. You didn't need to call me right now." I shakily say into my phone as quietly as I possibly can, with the way I am feeling at this very moment, when deep down all I want to do is scream.

"Are you flipping kidding me, please say you are joking Amber, have you found any more messages from her?"

"No, not yet. I'm too scared to look to be honest Millie, it was all right for me to think that he was cheating on me, but to actually see it in black and white is another matter. Now though I don't know if I want to know the truth, just finding out this girl is pregnant is hard enough. I am beside myself how could Jason do this to me. What's worse is how many of his mates know about it and do his family all know. I've been made to look like a laughing stock, Millie."

"Try to stay calm Amber, let's just take this one step at a time. First things first, why don't you put the woman's phone number into your own phone, so if Jason does get up and comes downstairs before you have had the chance to have a proper look. At least this way you have the woman's number and you can call her and ask her what's been going on with the both of them."

"Okay, that is actually a good idea. I will do that now. I don't know why I didn't think of that to be honest." It literally feels as though my mind has gone blank. I cannot seem to process anything. I'm in utter shock and maybe in a tiny bit of denial.

"Well for one you won't be thinking straight as your head will be all over the place to be fair. Right, what I want you to do now Amber, is see if there are any more messages from the same number."

As I go through the messages on Jason's phone, I notice there is quite a few and also shockingly a lot from a dating website. This goes a little way to explain why his pissing phone bill was so fucking high, he's been using those high-rate costing sites. I can't believe this as I am seeing more and more my blood starts to boil. The walls in the bathroom are starting to close in on me, I start to get anxious and then I start to hyperventilate. Then I come across a picture of the said girl. It's a picture of her in her kitchen, I presume, in just her underwear. I start crying as I stare at the photo of her, I am not usually the jealous type but she is gorgeous. There she was posing in her sexy lacy bra and French knickers, her ample chest pushed up and stuck out, her long brown hair cascading down her back whilst she has her index finger in her mouth, as if she is saying come and get me if you want me. Simply put she is sex on legs. From the look of the messages, it's been going on for a while and looks like it's really serious. I cannot control the tears any more, I feel sick to the stomach and then the penny drops. The two-timing bastard has been having his cake and eating it, he has been having sex with the both of us. Well actually we haven't had sex in the last two and a bit months, but even so. I feel dirty all of a sudden, thinking to myself that after he's been inside her then he has been in me. I feel betrayed and hurt.

"I need to get out of here Millie, I cannot stay here at the moment, I need to talk to her before I have this out with Jason."

"Come straight over to mine, just get what you need for a couple of days and stay with me here at mine."

"Thanks Millie, I think I will call her as well, whilst I walk over to your place. I just want to throw his phone at him, I don't care any more he cannot exactly get out of this and if I ring her before he does, he won't have the chance to get to her first to deny it or play it down."

"Good thinking Amber, I'm here for you and I'll see you soon."

"Yeah, I'll see you in a bit and Millie…"

"Yes?"

"Thank you and thanks for letting me stay at your place for a bit. I would be lost without you, and our friendship, it means the world to me."

"No worries hon, I feel the same, now hurry up and get your arse over here," Millie says to lighten the mood a bit.

Millie and I have known each other for so many years that we are literally like sisters and there is no place I would rather be than at hers right now, well apart from Pippa, she is like my surrogate mother since my mother passed away a few years ago and she stepped into that position.

I quickly run upstairs to my bedroom not caring what noises I make. I get together everything that I will need for a few days and bang it all into my overnight bag. Once I've got myself sorted, I go into the spare room and throw Jason's phone with perfect aim straight at his head. He wakes with a start, and the shock on his face when he realises what he has been hit with, his face goes a deathly pale grey colour. I hurriedly turn and run down the stairs, and as I am about to open the front door to leave, I hear Jason shout out, "WAIT AMBER, PLEASE I CAN EXPLAIN!" For one nanosecond, I think to myself I should wait and hear him out but then logic takes over. Without even looking over my shoulder I leave the house, slamming the door shut behind me.

As I start walking to Millie's I get out my phone and get the woman's number up and call it. It starts to ring, well I guess Jason hasn't got straight onto the phone to her. All of a sudden though as the woman's phone continues to ring, I start feeling all anxious and that ball in the pit of my stomach starts to build up, then the panic follows. After all that, I start to question myself. What am I going to say to this girl, does she know about me? How will she react to me ringing her up like this? Then before I can think any more, she answer's her phone.

"Hello," she says.

"Hi, erm... my name is Amber, you don't know me, well I don't think you do. However, I believe you know Jason," I say as casually as I can manage.

"Oh Amber, Jason's sister right, is he okay after our lovely surprise shock from the weekend? He was a bit stunned and a bit green when he left me yesterday."

"Shock, surprise? Sorry, but I have no idea what you are

35

talking about and not to sound stupid or anything but did you just say sister?"

Did I just hear that right she actually thinks I'm his sister... HIS SISTER... HIS FUCKING SISTER? I hear her suddenly have a little giggle to herself. What the fuck is going on?

"Sorry, but I don't know your name and what in the heavens name is so damn funny?" I ask starting to feel myself getting angry.

"Oh, sorry I'm Lexi, I would have thought that you would have known that, has Jason not told you about me? Why I'm laughing is because I was just remembering Jason's face when he saw that the pregnancy test was positive and that we were pregnant, he is so happy that he is going to be a father. Now he has had time to let it settle in, he was texting me last night talking off his joy. He explained to me shortly after we discovered that I was pregnant, that his ex-girlfriend had had an abortion behind his back and that he was so upset, that he never really quite got over it."

"Are you being serious right now? I actually can't believe what I am hearing," I say in response to what I have just heard.

"Look Lexi, is it? Listen I am doing my best to keep my cool here and trying not to lose my temper with you. First thing first though, I am not Jason's pissing sister for one thing, I am actually his girlfriend of five years, well actually that will not be the case for much longer once I have had it out with him, that I can promise you. Secondly, I want to know, in actual fact I NEED to know everything, how long it's been going on for and without the gory details please."

I think our connection has been disconnected because suddenly the conversation has gone quiet and for a spilt second, I actually think the girl has hung up on me.

"Hello... are you still there... hello... are you going to answer me or not, Lexi."

Has this bitch hung up on me? I start to think to myself once again. Then I start to hear a little sob coming down the phone from her side. Crap, I think to myself as a small part of me starts to feel sorry for this girl. As she is just as innocent as I am in this situation.

"Look I'm sorry Lexi, I know all this must have come as a shock to you, which I get truly I do. You must see it from my point of view as well, as I only just found out about you, Jason and the baby about an hour or so ago, if that even. Just to put you in the picture it wasn't Jason that told me either. I found out through looking through his phone, as I felt that something wasn't right and that he was hiding something from me. I need to know is the baby Jason's as well?"

"Ye... yes," she says through her sobs. "I'm so, so sorry, Amber. I had no idea; you have to believe me. Honestly, I was told that you were his sister and that he had moved into your place, as he couldn't afford to live where he was, since he was made redundant. With Jason being a nice guy and genuine to me, I had no reason to distrust him whatsoever, and as anyone would, you take it at face value."

The poor girl, that was the problem with Jason. He was a nice bloke, always doing anything for you without wanting anything in return. He would always put others before himself and on top of that he had the looks to go with it. You could say that he had the full package, well minus the cheating bastard part of him. It was understandable why she fell for him, that I could comprehend in my head. However, what I couldn't get my head around though, was why he would or did cheat on me in the first place. Where and when did it start going wrong? Had I pushed him away and if so, how? When did he literally stop loving me, and did he not find leading a double life exhausting? He could have sat me down and been upfront about the whole thing. Yes, I would have been angry and wonder what I had done wrong. I would have been extremely hurt and upset, and yes, there would have been a lot of crying, and yes the weaker side of me would have probably begged him to give our relationship a chance or another go. I am only human and a girl in love. Yes, I know that it would make me look pathetic and weak. However, knowing that he has led this double life and now has a secret child on the way, all those emotions of hurt, anger, pain, betrayal and lastly humiliation all turned into hate towards Jason. It brought to mind that famous saying that goes something like 'there is a very thin line between love and hate.' I never really understood it until now, only a couple of hours ago I really did love Jason even with all the troubles that we had been having recently and now, a couple of hours later, that love has literally turned into hate and I didn't want to set my eyes on Jason again.

"Lexi, just tell me how long it's been going on for please, that you owe me, regardless how innocent you may be in the situation. I just need to know for my own sanity, my own peace of mind and where I need to go from here."

"Well, we met via a dating website, lonely hearts in the local area. We sent a few phone texts here and there, then the phone calls followed from there, which then led to us both sending pictures, so we knew who we were looking for when we met up. I feel so uncomfortable talking to you about all this, it should really be coming from Jason don't you think? Especially knowing what I know now. I feel so bad, I really do."

"I wanted to get your side of the affair before I speak to Jason, as I want the truth and the facts. As I don't think I will get that from him, he will only give me half of the truth. How long has it been going on for, Lexi?" I ask frustratedly.

"It all started officially last year, when we met up on the August bank holiday for a long weekend, that was when we started sleeping together also, again Amber I am sorry but, you wanted to know."

I quickly worked it out in my head and counted the months down on my fingers.

"Seven months," I shout down the phone. "Seven bastard months." I respond in total shock. The conversation between us goes quiet for a few seconds whilst I allow that bit of information to sink in. There is one final question I need to know the answer to and this is going to hurt, but regardless, I need to know either way.

"One last thing I need to know Lexi, do you both love each other? Have you both actually said the words 'I love you' to one another?"

"Erm... yes, we have. We have also talked about Jason moving in with me now that we have the baby on the way."

I had no idea how I was to respond to that declaration. I still had a whole barrel of questions whizzing around in my head, but the one that came to mind was:

"So what are you going to do knowing what you now know?" I say back to her, whilst I'm trying to control the tears that are building up. Shit, I say to myself, get a grip of yourself

Amber, come on girl get your emotions under control. Once you get to Millie's then you can let it all out, until then get a grip of yourself.

"I want the three of us to be a proper family and I love Jason, I'm in love with him. I don't want my child being brought up in a broken family environment before it's even born."

"I'm sorry, but I cannot take any more of this conversation, it hurts too much. I just hope that it works out for you and Jason, he is all yours. I just hope for your sake and the baby's, that Jason doesn't do to you, what he has done to me when he gets bored." I finally say and without waiting for a reply I hang up the phone. I know that the final words were a cheap shot, but in truth I also meant them. If Jason has done it once what's to stop him from doing it again?

As I continue on my walk to Millie's, I start to replay the conversation again in my head. How the hell did I not see the signs, they were there? Was I that dumb and blind? I know they say that 'love is blind', but was I blinded that much? I try to go back and remember last August and that bank holiday weekend. I try to recollect what Jason did and then suddenly it comes back to me. He had told me that him and a few of the lads from work, were having a lads' long weekend away to Ibiza. I remember him saying that they will be leaving early on the Thursday morning, and were returning the Tuesday afternoon, if I remember correctly. I recall how much he was looking forward to it, so happy and excited, he also had a spring in his step as he left the house. I also recall him taking his passport, as he was doing that thing that people do when they go aboard "tickets, passport, money. Tickets, passport, money." So that makes me think… Whoa hold on a minute, was he actually going away on a romantic break with Lexi, instead of the lads' holiday that he made it out to be? There is only one way to find out and that's to ask Harry, Millie's cousin, as he used to work with Jason and he was supposed to have been one of the lads going on this so-called 'lads' holiday'. Also, Harry won't lie to me, we are pretty close as I have known him as long as I have known Millie. If anyone will know anything then it will be him. Plus, Harry has always had a bit of a soft spot for me as I have for him, but because off my close friendship with Millie I have never wanted to do anything with Harry that would jeopardise Millie's and my relationship. The last thing she would need was to be put into a difficult position between her best mate and her cousin.

CHAPTER FOUR

"Oh, hon, come here," Millie says as she pulls me in for a hug. We walk through to her kitchen and I can smell the fresh coffee bubbling away in her coffee machine. I smile to myself thinking how well she really does know me. As I go and take my usual seat at her kitchen island, that sits perfectly in the middle of the room, I feel utterly deflated as though the life has been sucked from me as well as heartbroken. Following that I have this sense of: this truly cannot be happening to me right now, my world as I know it has been rocked to its core and turned one hundred and eighty on to its axis. Once I have settled and Millie has put a mug of coffee in front of me, I sit there and just go into a daze and think to myself, how can my life have turned upside down so quickly? Then suddenly my eyes see a wave of a hand in front of my face, it's Millie's doing her best to bring me back to the here and now.

"You didn't hear a bloody word I just said then, did you?" Millie stares at me.

"Sorry Mil, I was just in my own little world then, sorry, what was it that you were saying?"

"Have you actually talked to the other woman yet? Oh, and before I forget, Carly and Pippa are both going to be popping round. Is that all right with you, I just thought that you would want your girlfriends around you at a time like this."

The thought that Millie had taken it upon herself to call

Pippa and Carly warms my heart, she truly is an extremely great friend and knows exactly what or who you need, even if you don't vocalise it yourself. Also, Millie must have thought to herself, that Pippa will be the one person that I will actually want by my side, well as well as herself at a time like this.

"Yeah, that's fine," is my only response that I can actually manage. I actually have no more words. I am physically shattered and I need to sleep. I've been awake now for more than twenty-four hours, and my brain feels frazzled.

"Is it okay if I take a quick shower, Millie, and then maybe a couple of hours sleep, before I have to go all over it again? I'm physically drained and I need to re-boot my batteries."

"Sure, no worries hon. You know where everything is just help yourself, and Amber, take all the time that you need. We will all be here for you when you wake up."

I just give her a weak smile and a slight nod of my head, get up from my seat leaving three quarters of my coffee and head towards her bedroom.

After I get everything I need from my overnight bag, I make my way across the landing to the bathroom, once inside I lock the door, put the shower on and close the lid on the toilet and sit there and cry in private. I cry like I have never cried before and I can actually feel my heart breaking into tiny pieces, it hurts, it hurts so much. Will anything ever be able to take this pain away? Finally, after I don't know how long, I manage to strip out of my clothes, throw them onto the floor in a heap and get under the welcoming hot water that awaits me from the shower. I just stand there, stood face first right underneath the showerhead so that my face takes the brunt of the water, whilst it washes away my warm salty tears. I do my best to control myself, but the pain is so overwhelming that I fall to the shower floor. I sit there whilst I hug my legs, tightly pushing my knees into my chest and finally I let my body succumb to my heartache and let the stream of tears flow, until my eyes start to sting and there are no more tears left to cry. Once I have shampooed and conditioned my hair and used Millie's expensive body oils and soaps and the water goes from hot to lukewarm, do I then get myself out of the shower.

Once I am dried and dressed into comfortable loungewear, I go to the mirror and take in my appearance. Oh boy, my reflection isn't the prettiest of sights at all, my eyes are red and really puffy looking, as well as a bad runny nose through the crying. It actually feels like I've had the world's worst hay fever attack, if that is even possible. To be honest and as much as I don't want to acknowledge it, I do feel a little better after having a good cry, however what I need now though is to sleep. So I quickly put on some face moisturiser and comb my hair and put it into a plait, I haven't even got the energy left to blow dry it, well at least I will have some nice waves when I wake up, if I do accomplish to get any sleep. I just hope that I can manage to switch off my brain.

Two and a quarter hours later of surprisingly undisturbed sleep and feeling somewhat rested, I get up and head to the kitchen and I can hear the girls chatting away. If there is one thing that I hate and that is being the vocal point for their conversation, I know that they love me in their own special individual ways and they care. I just wish that we didn't have to do this full stop. All the questions, the pity looks, treating me like I'm a delicate and fragile flower that will break. I hope to wake up from this nightmare and hope it's all a very, very bad dream. Obviously, I know that isn't possible, however, there isn't any harm in wishing, is there?

"Oh Amber, come here sweetheart," Pippa hurriedly gets up and quickly walks over to me and I fall into her embrace, whilst she hugs me and gently rubs my back. Pippa is older than us and was sort of a friend of my mother. The best way to explain Pippa really is she is like Mrs Doubtfire, always wanting to help you out and is always there for you, in your time of need, come rain or shine. Ever since the death of my mother, Pippa has been the mother that you didn't think you wanted, but in fact she was what you needed. Pippa took me under her wing and has been there ever since that awful day. I thank my lucky stars every day for Pippa and I love her as though she was my mother.

"You want a cup of coffee now Amber, or...?' Millie then starts walking towards her fridge and opens it and all behold a couple of seconds later she says, "Ta-da! Carly got a couple of bottles of wine on her way here."

"Well, I thought it may require wine, when you rang me up and told me the very little that you knew," Carly responded back to Millie.

"No thanks, just the coffee for now please. Cheers, Mil.," I smile to her. "And Carly, thanks for the wine too. I'm sure it will come in handy a little later on as a pain relief I can probably guarantee it," I tell her as I go over to give her a big hug. I actually haven't seen Carly for a few weeks, she is, as I would call her, a free spirit and only answers to herself. Not only does Carly like to sail into the wind and likes to take risks, she parties hard and boy does she like the men. Carly is pretty much like a dude when it comes to sex, she always has a different guy with her and she doesn't give a rat's arse what people say or how they judge her. That is what I love about her, she is so confident in her skin that she never lets the negative insults affect her, simply put Carly will stick two fingers up to the world and carry on with what she loves doing, as long as she isn't hurting anyone, then what does it matter?

The four of us sit round Millie's kitchen island in silence for a few seconds, the only thing that you can hear making a sound is the kitchen wall clock.

"Are you ready to tell us then what's happened or not Amber?" Pippa gently asks me, breaking the awkward silence and reaches to hold my hand, just like my mother would do when she saw me distressed. Heck, I miss my mum so terribly, I wish she was here now I could do with one of her bear hugs. I lost my mother suddenly nearly eleven years ago now, I was the one to find her on that horrific morning. It was through the week, a Tuesday morning, and as usual I let myself in with my key and I recall shouting out to her, 'Hi, Mum, it's only me! But there was no reply. As I went to check each room downstairs there was no sign of her or the fact that she had even got up. As usually I would have seen her breakfast pots in the sink. So I thought to myself I'll go and check to see if she was up, as I approached her bedroom door I felt this uneasy coldness trickle down my spine. As though a part of me feared something, I gave my head a little shake and I opened her bedroom door and peered inside. There I saw my mum in her bed, still tucked in all snug as a bug in a rug, still fast asleep.

"Come on, Mum, rinse and shine," I said in a little sing-song manner as I went to open her curtains. There was no sound nor movement. I remember walking round to her side of the bed and went to gently wake her but, as soon as I touched her, it felt like I was touching an ice cube. My mother was so cold and as I looked at her again, I noticed her deathly grey skin. Then the realisation hit me, I was looking at my mother's dead body. My brain couldn't compute it though, she still to my mind's eyes looked alive and just sleeping, but to touch her and the colour of her skin was saying something completely different. Mum had died in her sleep at some point through the night. My mother was taken away from this earth far, far too early. I didn't have the chance to say goodbye to her, tell her I loved her for the last time. Then I was trying to remember what were our last words to each other and I remembered that we had arranged to go shopping, then before we hung up, we both said love you, bye. Everyone does that though. I just wished we had more time together. If though you were going to die in any kind of way, then I suppose that is the nicest and kindest way to pass on. However not so much for the rest of us left behind, who have to go through all the stages of hurt, pain, anger, frustration, emptiness and most off all the sense of utter and complete loss. I still don't think I have really gotten over the shock of finding her like I did that terrible Tuesday morning. In a way Pippa kind of took over that motherly role in my life, she is the best thing I have to a mother, now.

I feel my eyes starting to go all moist again as I try to compose myself, looking up at my dear friends who are like family to me and realise how lucky I am.

"Come on pet, we're here for you. It's better out than bottling it all up," Pippa gently suggests to me. I give her a weak smile in return to her motherly words. So as the famous saying goes, I go for it, and rip the plaster off and go straight in.

"Well, the girl in question is called Lexi and I got quite a lot out of her." I wait a few seconds to let that settle in before I restart.

"So what did the bitch have to say for herself then?"

"Carly," me, Pippa and Millie all say in unison.

"Lexi is nothing of the sort and to be fair to her, I actually liked her, and also, I felt really sorry for the girl, as she did for me. All she kept saying was how sorry she was, she had absolutely no idea who I was. From what I could gather from the conversation I had with Lexi walking over here, was that she met Jason via the Internet, lonely hearts for the local area last year, went on a lovely romantic break last August bank holiday."

"Whoa, wait a minute there, Amber. How could that be? Wasn't that not the weekend the lads all went away because, if I also remember rightly, but weren't us girls planning on going to Blackpool the same time?" Millie says to me a little confused.

That about sums it all up really, doesn't it? Confusion all around us.

"Yeah, well it was all lies, a cover story. Which actually reminds me of something, I need to speak to your Harry about it Millie. He was meant to be going away with them on this so-called lads' weekend. Be interesting to get his point of view of what he knows. Anyway, carrying on, they have been together since last year. So if I have done the maths right, the cheating bastard has been cheating on me for seven months, seven fucking months. Sorry for the language Pippa. Oh, and to add insult to injury, and to put that beautiful little red cherry on top of the bastard cake, they are very much in love, they have discussed that Jason is moving in with her and she is pregnant with Jason's love child. To put the final nail into the coffin, apparently Lexi thought I was Jason's sister. He made out to her, that when he lost his job, he couldn't afford his place any more and he had to move in with me 'his sister'. You know what, Millie, I think I will have that glass of wine now."

I put my elbows onto the worktop of the kitchen island, and rested my chin into my hands and I just space out. Trying my best to recount the past year and seeing if I had missed something, trying to recall any red flags that were flying around straight in front of my damn eyes. Even so though we were still having sex up until a couple of months or thereabouts. He even kept that side of our relationship up. An overwhelming emotion of sickness consumes me, thinking that he was dipping his nib into the two of us. How could the worthless bastard do that? Then another thought comes to mind, which makes me think that I now need to go and get an STD test, because if Lexi is pregnant, then he wasn't using protection with her or with me, as I was on the pill.

"Shit Amber, that's a lot of information you have just bombed us with. Stupid question, but how are you feeling?" Millie questions me. I don't even respond back, as I think the tears are doing all the talking for me. All I do is give my shoulders a shrug. The lovely amazing Pippa does what Pippa does best, she simply gets up from her seat and gently takes me into her arms and comforts me whilst she rocks me like a baby. No words are necessary and she lets me cry to release my pain.

"Five years of my life I have given that bloke, five damn years and this is my reward for all the hard work and effort

I've put into it. Jason was meant to be one of the good ones. I'm thirty and I'm going to have to start again."

"Well, whenever you are ready to get back on that horse, I have plenty of single lad mates I could hook you up with. To get over someone is to get under someone and all that."

"Carly, not everyone is sex mad like you," Millie laughs at Carly whilst giving her a playful jab in the arm.

"What I think Amber needs," starts Pippa after she has given Carly one of her scary glares, "is a girly trip away and I have got a couple of free tickets to the West End musical *Wicked* in London. I can't go myself and it would be such a waste if no one used them. Millie, why don't you and Amber, go, it's the back end of May. It's on a Tuesday evening, just before the last May bank holiday."

"Oh Pippa, that is so generous of you." I can't help but to hug her. I have always wanted to see *Wicked* and it has had so many great reviews.

"Are you sure though? I can always give you some money towards the tickets. At this moment though I'm not sure if I want to go. Is it okay if I think about it for a bit and let you know?"

"Don't be silly child, I don't want anything for them. You think about it, but let me know if you want them or not, if not then I can give them to someone else." Pippa gently taps my hand. "However, if you do want them, they're all yours, that smile alone is payment enough."

As we all start to talk about London and what me and Millie could do, my phone vibrates in my pocket signalling that I have received a message. I slip of my chair, excuse myself, and and quietly go into the lounge. Shutting the door behind me, I reach for my phone. I see that the text is from Jason, I don't know whether to ignore it and just delete it straight away, but there is that tiniest part of me that is clinging on to something, what that is I don't know. The latter part of my reasoning wins and I open the message from him:

I am so, so sorry Amber, truly I am,
Lexi said that you had called. It
should have been me to tell you
everything, it wasn't fair to put
either you or Lexi in that position.
I'm sorry that you had to find out
this way. I do think that we should
talk though, don't you?
J X

I re-read his words and for the first time I don't actually feel my eyes welling up. To be fair to me though, after all the tears I have shed, I could have made my own little personal stream. I am actually though all cried out and to be honest at this moment all I am feeling is numbness. Yes, that about sums it up for me, I am sat here feeling void of all emotions and numb from the pain. I mean what else is there really left to say and what can he add to what I already know? I don't want to hear his sorrys, I don't want to hear anything from him. I hit the reply button to send him a text back:

There is really nothing left to say
is there Jason? I have heard
everything. Lexi told me more,
then what you would of ever

have told me. You are a
spineless coward and a cheating
bastard. So no we do not need to
talk. What I need from you is to
pack all your shit up and leave my
house, I am going to give you a
couple of days to move out, that
gives you plenty of time. Once
you have finished, you can post
my keys back through the letter
box.

Once I have sent that message to him, I go into my contacts and delete his number, then I go and delete every bit of contact between the two of us, from messages to emails and photos, so I don't have any form of evidence of him on my phone. As I know that in a couple of weeks or a few months down the line and I get pissed and I know I will end up drunk calling him. I need to close this chapter once and for all. No looking back or even going back if truth be told. Jason is and always will be a part of my history, and that is where he shall stay, forever in my past.

CHAPTER FIVE

After I have spent a couple of nights at Millie's and had the girls all around me and quite a few bottles of wine between us, as well as a bottle of gin for the four of us — well mainly Carly and me shared it. It is time for me to return to my real world and face the reality and go home. Plus, I really do need to get back as I am back at work in a couple of days and I have my work uniform to get washed, dried and ironed as well as other chores, like washing the bedding to get rid of all smells of Jason. I give Millie a huge hug, thank her for all she has done for me over the last couple of days and say my goodbyes and take a lovely walk back home.

The sun is blazing outside, the temperature has picked up and there isn't a cloud in the sky, you can feel the heat beating down on you. I really do enjoy this time of year, where you can put all your dark chunky jumpers and the rest of your winter clothing to the back of your wardrobe and your bright spring/summer clothing comes to the front of your closet. You put away all your shoes and boots, and out, come the flip-flops and sandals. It's time to get your skin all nice and bronzed with the little micro-balls of fire from the sun heating up and slightly burning your skin. Time for them freshly pedicured toes to be let out into the glorious sunshine. In my opinion I think everyone looks so much happier and healthier in the summer, no doubt from all the extra vitamin D from the rays of the sun. I have also noticed that people tend to look after themselves more in the summer months, maybe that's because it is always too hot to eat anything heavy. Usually all I want to eat is a sandwich or just a bowl of cereal. You tend to get yourself out a lot more to take in a little extra exercise, whether that's to go for a jog, a nice country bike ride, a lovely summer's evening walk, or the best of them all, is a walk to the beach and go for a swim in the sea. I guess the lovely evening walks I will be doing alone from now on, then I get an idea I could get myself a dog, at least I will have some company, but then with my job pattern that wouldn't work out well and it sure won't be fair on the little furry creature, stuck indoors all the time, with hardly any exercise. Oh well, nice idea while it lasted. As I continue on my walk which I am greatly enjoying weirdly enough, I listen to the birds. I simply love the different sounds of the birdsongs and I don't know if you have noticed, but all the different species of birds and their songs, complement each other. My favourite bird sound though has to be the wood pigeon, however you don't really hear it throughout the day as much as the rest of the birds. I will always hear them making their cooing sounds in the morning, when I sit in my garden with my first cup of coffee of the day and again when I am home in the evenings around dusk time. I do always look forward to hearing the sound of the wood pigeons, I have found their song or cooing very soothing on many occasions and it always puts a smile on my face.

Once I have reached my house and let myself in, I just stand there in my lounge, with my arms wrapped around my chest to give myself a hug. Wow. The evidence is so overwhelming all around me of the fact that Jason had once lived here with me and was now gone. All the gaps and spaces are huge, from the CD tower in the corner of the room, the DVD shelves, all his silly little ornaments as well as some of his slightly larger ones and all his family photos that have been removed from the walls, fireplace and the windowsill. It's all gone, everything, the life we shared obliterated and turned into ash and been blown away in the wind until nothing is left to show for what was once there. Astonishing isn't it, that in a blink of an eye, things changed and you know that they will never be the same again? What's even weirder is knowing that in that space of forty-eight hours all Jason's belongings that were here, are now sitting prettily in Lexi's home.

I slowly make my way into the kitchen to make myself one of my herbal teas, as I really do need to go on a detox plan especially after all the alcohol I have managed to consume recently. As I turn to leave though something catches my eye, there on one of my kitchen cupboard doors, is taped an envelope with my name on it, in Jason's handwriting. I haven't the emotional strength to face it, I take it down and throw it away into the garbage, I want to keep to my promise that I made myself. I will have nothing and I don't want to see or hear anything from Jason ever again. That man will get no more of my time or energy, he has had enough.

Once I have my cup of lemon and ginger tea ready and put the washing machine on, I go and get into my favourite comfortable slops, get the chocolate ice cream from the freezer that I stashed away for emergencies and get myself comfy on my sofa. My one and only decision is should I binge watch *Sex and The City* or, watch all three *Bridget Jones Diary* movies, back-to-back. Both of these are my go-to programmes/movies when I feel sad or lonely. I finally opt to watch *Bridget Jones*, you tell me which woman cannot relate to Bridget. We, well, actually I cannot speak for every woman, but for me, I want the same as the wonderful Bridget. We all want to find ourselves our own perfect Mr Darcy. However though, we always seem to find ourselves with the typical Daniel Cleavers of the world. The spineless, worthless cowards and cheating bastards, who have no conscience whatsoever and only think of themselves and their penises. Right now, at this very moment in time, that is the category I would differently put Jason into. Then I start to wonder to myself, did he ever spare me a moment's thought at all? Did he ever once feel guilty? Or worse still, did he enjoy hurting me and then meeting up with his mates and bragging about what he was getting away with? Giving them all a laugh at my expense and humiliation. Fucking dickhead. Bag of worthless shit. A sudden thought hits me like a firebolt, I wonder to myself could Harry actually be my Mr Darcy? The amount of missed opportunities we've had. The last one was just before Jason came onto the scene and asked me out. Crap, where the hell did that come from? Talk about random, it came out of nowhere. What people don't know about me and Harry, is that we have shared on many occasions, a few cheeky kisses. Yes, many of them were all drunken snogs, in fact, as I come to think of it properly, they have all been drunken kisses we have shared, to finish off a pretty perfectly good evening out, and let's not forget all the flirting that has passed between the two of us. Obviously, that all stopped when I got with Jason as I'm not that kind of girl. I give my head a little shake and have a chuckle to myself, and I press play and leave my world and for a few hours I go into Bridget Jones's world and try to forget everything.

CHAPTER SIX

The next couple of weeks go by, without too much of a hitch. To be honest I have kept myself busy with work, working plenty of overtime. My mum would always in the kindest kind of way drum it into me when I was a lot younger, that if you were upset about something, or if something happens to you, then don't wallow in self-pity. Never let that pit of despair grab a hold of you, always keep yourself busy and keep your mind focused on different areas of your life. Guess what? She was bloody right. If she was here now, I know exactly what she would say, 'Well, dear, mothers always know best.' I haven't really had time to think about anything other than my job in hand, the only time I've been home is to sleep, eat when I remember to and to shower. I feel as though I have gone on the post-break-up diet and I have lost a little over half a stone. I'm starting to look gaunt and exhausted, and really ill within myself. Fortunately for me though, I have the coming weekend off and I am going to Millie's for a BBQ. It has all been arranged for the first May bank holiday weekend of the year. Weather permitting, I will be spending Saturday recuperating and relaxing in the garden sunbathing with a good book. On Sunday it's all round to Millie's for a BBQ and in the evening, she will be getting her chimney fire pit out for a fire and I will be spending the night at hers, followed on Monday we will go to our favourite cafe called Wide Awake Cafe for our traditional annual hangover breakfast.

I've tried my best in the house filling in the spaces and gaps that Jason's things have left behind, by moving my own CDs, books, DVDs, photo frames as well as the furniture. No matter what I do though it just doesn't feel right at all. What I think I need to do is to have a proper complete household makeover. Redecorate the whole place right through and maybe new fixtures and fittings, which will give a new feel to the place. I don't want to make it too girly though, I like the idea of white walls painted white throughout the house, in the bedrooms, hallway and stairs and the lounge to have thick grey carpets and the kitchen and bathroom to have that really expensive thick lino also in a slate-grey affect. I want no reminders of Jason ever being there. I'm going to treat myself to a new sofa for the lounge and a new bed and mattress for my room, curtains and instead of blinds I'm going to get the professionals in to put up shutters. Yes, time to spend some of my hard-earned money, that I have saved.

It's Friday evening and I'm shattered, it has been one hell of a week at work. The hospital I work at, St Vincent's, is in a bit of a shambles, the board need to do something and pull their fingers out of their arses. There are never enough beds for patients, to make room for new patients, we have to send patients home far too early, and get the community nurse team to follow up and take over their care in the community. Some patients have to go onto wards that don't specialise in the treatment that some individuals require. It is becoming a joke, I became a nurse to help and care for people and to get to know my patients. All I'm seeming to be doing is sitting at the ward desk and filling in paperwork, like I work in office administration. Once I have spent the best part of thirty to forty-five minutes completing my patient paperwork and getting them admitted onto the ward, in that time the patient has been seen by the doctors and assessed by the time I have finished. Then it's literally time for them to be moved to an available bed onto another ward. That's sometimes, the most stressful thing working on the Emergency Admissions Unit (EAU). Once you have finished with one patient, by the time you look up, as quick as an hour, that patient has been moved elsewhere and you have a new patient to admit onto the ward, so you have to start all over again. When it's been a week like what I've just had, it makes me want to look for a new job because I don't enjoy what I'm doing any more.

So after the long week I've had, I have a cold glass of wine and I'm now sitting in my little bit of paradise and on my swing seat. Finally managing to unwind and relax and doing what I love to do in the evening and that is listening to the birds. I can smell the aromas coming from the neighbours' gardens. There are a few BBQs being lit tonight and it tantalises my tastebuds and my mouth starts watering, which sends a signal to my stomach because it starts to growl like an angry bear wanting to be fed. I head into my kitchen to check out what I have that is edible in the fridge. I have enough ingredients for a small salad, I go to the cupboards to see what I have in them, nothing, apart from a sad lonely little tin of tuna. It still comes in handy as I open it and drain the oil and tip the tuna onto of my salad. I top up my wine glass and go back outside and eat my dinner and relax for the rest of the evening.

The following day and feeling much more rested, I open my curtains and it is a glorious scorching day. So in respect to the day, I decide to put on my short denim shorts and a bikini top, and head downstairs to make my morning coffee. I really cannot function properly without that first hit of caffeine. Once I have the coffee machine filled and switched it on, I give Millie a call.

"Hi Millie, it's only me, what you up to today?"

"Oh, nothing much, just cleaning up after fucking men, I had an unexpected house guest last night and his mates came round. Looks like he'll be staying with me for a bit. Only if he starts to clean up after himself the lazy bastard, honestly Amber it actually feels like I have a teenage son living at home and it's only been one night. 'HARRY!'" Millie shouts. 'Come and clean your fucking shit up, this is no fucking dosshouse for you to crap all over, show me some respect'. Sorry Amber, right I'm back."

"Hey no worries, sounds like it's a bit stressful your side," I laugh down the phone to her.

"No kidding, Harry has had a falling out with his new girlfriend, he can't go to his parents, because my aunt and uncle are in Mexico for their yearly holiday. So muggins here, was the only person he could come to."

"Oh Millie, I feel for you. Mexico though, nice for some. Do you want me to go and I can give you a bell a little bit later if that's better for you?"

"Oh Amber, could you? That would be great, sure you don't mind though?"

"No worries hon, I call you back later," with that we hang up.

I send Carly a quick text to see if she was around and see what she is up to. I don't bother with Pippa as I know that she is visiting her sister who lives down south, the Isle of Wight if I remember correctly. I hear back from Carly pretty much straight away, no surprise though she is busy with her new bloke of the week. So I take this rare opportunity to laze around and sunbathe in the back garden.

So here I am, the first bank holiday weekend of May, all alone laying in my garden, sunbathing and listening to love songs on my iPhone and reading Charlotte Brontë's *Villette*. When I start to think to myself, I am going to be alone for the rest of my life, aren't I.

As some of the songs I'm listening to catch my attention I put my book down. When you listen to some of the lyrics to many love songs and you hear how the guy sings about the woman he loves, you think or say to yourself, that's what I want, is it really too much to ask for? My eyes fill with tears as I hear the amazing John Legend singing one of his famous songs *All Of Me* and I start to think how lucky his wife is. Why can't there be a few more John Legends in the world and if there was, please could one be directed in my direction with a helping hand to find me?

The neighbours must think I am a right saddo. At least I haven't got my music too loud and I'm not blubbering like a lovesick teenager, but I am pretty close. Both my neighbours have small families and as I hear the young children laughing and playing, shouting to their mums and dads to come outside and play with them. Then out of the blue as I hear the endearing words the parents say in response weakens me, because I realise, that at the age of thirty, I don't have that and I'm not even close to getting it. Whilst listening to all the happy activities going on around me, unknown to everyone else, as I am shielded from anyone seeing me thanks to the conifers on both sides that hides me and my garden. I am quietly weeping because, deep down if I was really truthful to myself, that is exactly what I want. A family of my own and a strong partnership where you feel you can beat anything together. A partnership that is fifty-fifty, straight down the middle. I want what everyone says is stressful at times but also rewarding all the time. As I quietly listen, I wonder to myself when will it be my turn, or will I ever get a turn at that kind of blissfulness?

It's Sunday morning and I'm waiting for the taxi to pick me up to go over to Millie's. I have far too much to carry, mainly two crates of lagers and five bottles of wine to name a few things, so walking to Millie's is out of the question. It's going to be a great day with the girls and apparently now that Harry is staying at Millie's himself, he will be there too with a couple of his mates. After a restless and shitty night and to be honest feeling pretty low in mood and in myself, all I want to do today is eat a lot, drink plenty and forget all my worries and have a bloody fantastic time.

"The cavalry has arrived and she has brought plenty of goodies, bottles of wine, crates of lager and a couple of shopping bags. Boys, come and give Amber a hand, will you?" Pippa shouts over her shoulder as she comes to help me with the bags.

"I thought you were down south, visiting your sister?" I say in shock and pleasantly surprised.

"I came back early darling, now come and give me a hug," Pippa sweetly smiles to me, and opens her arms, as I walk into her embrace and take the comfort she is offering me, and instantly feeling at ease, as I always do when it comes to being wrapped in Pippa's bosom.

"All right Amber-licious, long time no see," Harry says in his typical flirty way, as he walks past us to get all the goodies out of the trunk of the taxi.

"Hi Harry," I respond with a slight watery smile. "You're looking good. Listen I need to talk to you about something later, when you have some time." I pull away from Pippa and get the money from my purse for the taxi and hand it to Harry.

"Here's the money for the cab, cheers Harry."

"No bother, now go and get your skinny arse in there, Millie is in the kitchen, making some kind of honey salad dressing."

As me and Pippa make our way down the side of Millie's towards her back garden, she pulls me to a stop and wants to know how I am really doing and managing to cope. I simply told her the truth about working like a dog and about my quiet, lonely, tearful despair of a day, yesterday. I explained to her that yes, I was still hurting and I need to deal with my moaning period the best way I can. Today though I told her, all I want to do is have fun, get tipsy and forget my problems for a bit. Pippa then surprised me by saying that she wanted to come to mine in a couple of days, as she had something important that she wanted to put across to me and she hoped that I would take the opportunity that she was offering me, but she wouldn't pressure me either way, and the decision had to be mine and mine alone. To say I was intrigued was an understatement and on top of that, I'm not to say anything to anyone until we have both talked.

"Promise me now, Amber, not a word to anyone, that is all I ask of you, for now," Pippa asks. I didn't say a word but, just nodded my head in a slightly confused and dazed manner, as I had no other way to react to such secretive behaviour. I was, however, fascinated and bemused as this wasn't the typical behaviour of Pippa.

"Oh, great, Amber, you're here. You couldn't give us a hand in the kitchen, please? I have Carly making the salad, the coleslaw and the potato salad are all done. Harry is taking over the BBQ so I have marinated the meats, all I need to figure out is how to do your salad dressing, Amber."

"Well, that's easy enough, all you need is balsamic vinegar, honey and Dijon mustard," I happily tell her.

"Dijon mustard? No wonder it doesn't taste right, I've been using bloody English mustard."

"No worries, I'll pop round to the shop and get some. Carly, do you need anything, actually does anyone need anything?"

Everyone just chorused the same reply, "No thanks, Amber."

"Actually," Millie shouted over towards Harry, "Harry go with her, and get some cigs please, oh, and I want the change back this time."

"Come on then Amber, you heard the boss lady. The sooner we get there, the sooner we get back and get this party started."

I know why Millie has set this up, she is one sly clever fox, but in a really good way and I appreciate this opportunity that she has manged to offer us. I can now talk to Harry without anyone trying to eavesdrop on our conversation.

"As much as Jason was a good mate of mine and deep down he is a good lad, but in my opinion I didn't think he was good enough for you, or that you were an ideal couple, come to that."

"What the hell do you mean by that," I angrily ask him. Talk about winding someone up, who has already been punched to the ground.

"All I'm saying Amber is that you deserved someone a lot better, someone who should've treated you right."

"No, you have no right to say that, we were together for five years damn you, that counts for something Harry."

"Okay, look I'm sorry and I'm sorry if I've upset you, but like you have just said yourself, it only lasted five years. If you were both suited to each other, each other's soulmates then wouldn't you be together for all eternity and all that crap?"

"Okay then, tell me one thing Harry as you seem to know everything, did you know what was going on?"

I realise as I wait for his reply that I am holding my breath. Of all people to know, please, please don't say that Harry knew all along.

"Don't do this to yourself, Amber, what good is it going to do now that you know everything?"

"DID YOU KNOW!" I raise my voice angrily.

"Yes, Jason told me a couple of months ago. I told him what I thought of him and the hurt that it was going to cause you. I even told him how he didn't deserve you, especially after the first time I covered for him. We had a huge fight, which ended up with the two of us falling out and we haven't spoken since."

"Hold on, what the hell did you just mean then? You said after the first time. How many times has Jason done this to me?"

"Shit, after Millie told me you knew everything in regard to Jason's cheating, I just jumped to the conclusion that Jason at long last had been open and honest about the dirty business."

"Jason told me jack, Harry, I've found out myself and got the rest from Lexi. How many more times were there and who were the girls? Tell me now, I want to know everything."

"There was just one other occasion and it lasted three months, that's all I know, I promise you, Amber."

"Do you know who it was?"

"Geez Amber, don't do this to yourself please, I'm begging you. You of all people doesn't need to know. You've already had to go through so much, you don't need any more heartache."

"If you have any respect, for the little bit of friendship we have left, Harry, then you better tell me."

"It was Carly," Harry says frustratedly whilst running his hand through his hair.

I stand on the spot as though I have been frozen there, trying to compute what I have just heard. Then as though my body is acting in its own accord I start lashing out at Harry and shouting at him calling him a lying bastard, wanting him to take it all back. Harry didn't bat an eyelid, he quickly took hold of me, and held me tight in his arms so I couldn't move, as though I was being held in a straitjacket. I couldn't believe it, one of my close friends. So not once but twice I was betrayed by my ex-boyfriend and now hearing that he had cheated on me with one of my friends, has wounded me in one of the worst possible ways, with her betrayal. All the times she has been there, a shoulder to cry on, to bitch to and to let off some steam in respect to my relationship with Jason, then a thought occurs to me.

"Did Mil—"

"No, Millie knew nothing of it. Come on, you two are so close, you are literally like sisters. If she knew she would've told you Amber, that's why I kept my mouth shut, I didn't want to see you hurt, it pains me now to see you like this."

Harry though should have told me sooner, I am furious with him and keeping Jason's betrayal from me, for as long as he has done, doesn't escape my notice either. He was the one man I thought I could truly depend on, but yet again I've been hit in the face by reality.

I tell Harry to go to the shop and get what was needed as I about turned and headed back to Millie's, contemplating to myself how best to handle the situation. Once I get back to Millie's, everyone is in the garden laughing and joking around. At that moment I see Carly acting her usual flirty self with Adam and Joe, a couple of Harry's mates, laughing at something one of them had just said, whilst she was running her fingertips up Joe's arm who I knew was dating someone. Seeing that, it made my blood boil. I go to the kitchen and pour myself a glass of wine and down half of it and go back into the garden with a determined look on my face.

"Amber, you all right sweetheart?" Pippa asks me.

Ignoring her I continue walking towards my target.

"Amber, whoa what's up? Where's Harry," says Millie.

Once I have reached Carly, I look her square in the eyes and without thinking too much about it, I throw the rest of my drink in her face.

"Whoa, you silly cow. What the hell was that for? Man, you really do have a screw loose in that brain of yours, you stupid bitch."

"Don't you dare talk to her in that manner." I look over my shoulder to see who had just said that and I see Harry at the garden fence with a shopping bag, looking at Carly with a dark scowl on his face. The bloke must have ran back from the shops.

"Will someone tell me what the devil is going on, right now?" Millie shouts out.

"Why don't you enlighten the group Carly, come on everyone is waiting patiently, this is what you like isn't it? All the attention solely on you. Tell them, or should I?"

"I've really no idea what the hell you are talking about Amber," Carly says in that annoying cocky way of hers, where you literally want to punch her in the face, just to knock the smug grin of it.

"She knows, I've just told her. Well to be fair to me, I thought she already knew, after a small misunderstanding, I was told that Jason had told her everything," Harry calmly responds back to Carly.

As I look back at Carly. I notice the colour drain from her face and she starts to stutter.

"I'm s…s… so… sor… sorry, Amber."

"For the last time will someone tell me what the fuck is

going on?" Millie once again loudly raises her voice angrily

"I'll tell them shall I. Carly here, my so-called friend, also had a three-month affair with Jason behind my back. What was it Carly, had you run out of men to sleep with so you started on the ones that were taken? Or did you not give a rat's arse who you were doing any more, as long as you got some."

Silence fell all around me and now all eyes were on Carly, watching her as her back was up against the wall and trying to figure a way out of the situation, she now found herself in.

"Please tell me this isn't true."

"I'm sorry Pippa, I wish I could, but I can't." Carly replied, with no remorse or shame. Before I knew what was happening Millie is up in Carly's space and slaps her right across the face.

"You bitch, how could you do that to someone you say you care about? I thought you were many things, Carly, but this, this is despicable and heartless. All them times you've been there hearing Amber pour her heart out. All those negative comments you gave her back… shit, it all makes sense now."

"Carly, I think it would be best if you left now," Harry says to her, as Pippa walks towards me and puts a motherly protective arm around my shoulders.

"Just answer my question, Carly," I ask her. "Why Jason? It's not like you ran out of men to sleep with. Why him? And was it worth sacrificing our friendship for?"

"It was a drunken mistake."

I laugh bitterly. "A drunken mistake, that that lasted three fucking months."

"Look I can't explain it or my reasoning behind my logic, and yes, at times I did feel a little guilty. Also, I was jealous at the same time, because I fell in love with Jason and I still love the guy. However, he never felt the same way as he said that he only loved you. What he saw in me was a friend with great benefits, so every time the two of you argued or had a falling out, he would come to me, and forget."

"So all that time that you were bad mouthing him…?"

"I was hoping that you would listen to me and what I was saying, hoping that I had put enough negative thoughts into your head and you would finish with him. Then maybe after coming back to me, he would see me in a different light and give us a shot."

I am so angry, upset and frustrated all at once, I can't have it out with Jason as I have deleted all trace of him from my life. So Carly is getting the brunt of my anger and as the red mist distends, I go to attack her. Before I know it though, Harry is pulling me back before I can reach her.

"Don't, Amber, she isn't worth it."

"Let go of me Harry, NOW."

"No, I won't allow you to do this to yourself. I will not let you harm her either. Don't let her win Amber, the only one that will end up suffering in the end is you because, if I allow you to attack her, then you have given her the upper hand and she will report you to the police and you will end up being charged with GBH. Honestly Amber listen to me, she isn't worth it. You are better than this."

Millie at this point speaks up for me.

"I want you to get the hell out of my house now Carly, I cannot stand to look at you and don't you think we are friends after this. All you do is take what you want, when you want it, without thinking of the consequences of your actions. Now piss off, you're not wanted around here."

Carly quickly runs into the kitchen crying and grabs her bag, and just as she is about to leave through the gate, she turns round and looks at us all and says, "You know what, if I had to relive that part of my life again, I wouldn't change a damn thing. I would still have shagged Jason senseless; I have no regrets."

I try to go for her again but, Harry is far quicker than me and holds me back.

"You're a funking lunatic, Amber, no wonder you can't keep hold of a man if this is your behaviour and they need to look towards carefree girls like me." As Carly walks away, she stops suddenly and looks over her shoulder, her glare directed at me and she speaks. "Oh, and one more thing. The reason Jason also looked elsewhere is because he was looking for adventure and excitement in the bedroom. Not the boring and dull sex that you offered. What was it he said, again? Ah, that was it, all Amber does is lie there, it's like having sex with a plank of wood she's that stiff. Oh, and you were only willing to do one position. Whereas I offered him, hot, filthy exciting sex of his life. You see with me anything goes, sex toys, any position and ALL my sexual holes were at his disposal. I gave him what you couldn't. Maybe you should look into taking some lessons at a sex class and learn a few things," Carly said tartly. With her final words said, she turned and left, disappeared.

I fall to the floor in a massive heap, feeling the worst form of humiliation I have ever experienced in my life. I just wanted the ground to open up and swallow me whole, I wanted everyone to stop staring at me, waiting for my reactions to come to the surface. It was that flight or fight situation you hear of and at this moment in time I wanted to run from everyone and hide from the world. I didn't want to be around anyone and I needed to get out of here and away from all the pitying looks on people's faces. I had that feeling again even though I was in the open air outside, it still felt like the walls were closing in on me and my heartbeat was slowly raising, my hands were starting to go clammy and the beating drum in my head was increasing. I needed to get the hell out of here before I crumbled to tiny little pieces. With my decision made I slowly get up from the floor and look at Millie.

"I'm sorry, Mil, but I need to go. I've had all the attention I can cope with for one day. I need to go and lick my wounds."

"Amber, don't go please. Look, at least stay for the BBQ and get some food in you."

"I can't Millie, please I need to go," I say as I feel my eyes start to well up, like a dam ready to burst its banks. I do my best to get my emotions under control.

"Pippa, can you take me home please?"

"Sure I can, come on, let's get your things and get you back to yours, Okay?"

"Thanks, Pippa," I say as I go and fetch my things from the kitchen, and on my way out, I grab a couple bottles of wine.

"You don't mind do you, Millie?"

"Bloody hell, don't be silly, of course I don't mind. You brought most of them anyway."

"Thanks, and thanks for having my back."

"What else did you expect me to do Amber? Come on we're like sisters. If anyone hurts you then they hurt me and then they have to face the both of us."

"And vice versa." I smile back at her and go to hug her

goodbye.

"I'll ring you later, okay?"

"Okay, hon, you know where I am if you need me."

As me and Pippa reach the front of Millie's, I hear the sound of running footsteps.

"Amber, wait up." I spin round in shock and surprise to see Harry jogging up to us. Before I know it, he has his arms around me and hugs me tightly.

"Take care of yourself, you hear me? Oh, and I'm so sorry for ruining your bank holiday through opening my big month."

"It's all right Harry, well actually it isn't okay, but you know what I mean. None of this is your fault Harry, remember that. Look, I'll see you around."

With that I turn away and me and Pippa walk back to mine.

CHAPTER SEVEN

I don't remember much of my walk home, it was like I had shut my mind away from everything around me. I'm in a complete daze and feeling completely numb, ashamed and totally humiliated. Surprising really, isn't it? How much a day can change, who would have thought this was going to happen when I woke up this morning? You wake up all happy, relaxed and raring to go and really excited for your day to begin, and it finishes with the wind taken out of your sails. Like you have been sucker punched and winded, it came so quickly that you didn't have the time to prepare or the opportunity to defend yourself. All you could do is stand there and take the swings that are coming at you, or you can act on impulse, you act on the information and the surroundings you have been given.

"What did I ever do to the pair of them, to warrant this kind of betrayal from people who are meant to care about you, Pippa? I'm struggling to get my head around it all. The hatred in Carly's voice when she was humiliating me in front of everyone. Coming out with all that vile, nasty crap, which is all lies by the way, just in case you were wondering. Would Jason really have spoken about something so private and personal? I just don't know anything any more. I can't even trust my own judgement." I cry, not giving a rat's arse who sees me. Yes, okay I am feeling really sorry for myself, I've a right considering the circumstances.

"Now you listen to me, Amber Marie Smith, do not allow them two worthless pieces of vermin to get under that pretty skin of yours. Do not allow them to do this to you. Remember you are the injured party in this sorry mess, they've done this to you, not the other way round."

"You know what Pippa? I've not got the energy or the strength to do this all again. I'm sick and so tired of being the one always getting hurt. It is best to hold people at arms-length, and not allowing them in, by doing that at least I will be safeguarding my heart. My pride has taken a huge hit, well never again, I won't allow it. I cannot face the feeling of pain, betrayal and hurt like this again."

At this outburst Pippa stops and grabs hold of my arm, turns me around to face her and with such a stern, meaningful, don't-mess-with-me look. Once I have the control to look her squarely in her lovely grey-blue eyes, she gracefully takes my face into her hands and goes on to speak.

"Now you listen to me, yes, your confidence may have taken a hit and of course you're hurting right now, but that pain will pass I promise you that Amber. Shutting yourself off and closing your heart from ever loving again, well my dear, you're only hurting yourself in the long run. A life without love isn't a life at all, that's all I'm saying." I take that in for a few seconds, as Pippa quickly checks her watch and slowly, I see her frown lines appear on her forehead. "Sorry Amber, but I need to get off. But I will be back to check on you in a couple of days, to see how you are doing. Oh, and there is that matter I want to talk to you about."

"Don't you want to discuss it now?"

"No pet, you are not in the right frame of mind at this precise moment in time."

"As long as you're sure. And Pippa, thanks for the pep

talk."

"No thanks necessary, all I ask of you is to eat properly, rest up and try your best to get a good night's sleep."

"I'll try my best, that's all I can promise I'm afraid."

We give each other a kiss and a hug and we say our goodbyes. Here I am once again all on my lonesome, maybe that's for the best though. At least this way I won't be bringing anyone else down with my low mood and my self-pity. Once I have closed the front door, I go upstairs to my bedroom, lay on my bed and curl up in the foetal position and release all the built-up emotions that I have been keeping in. The floodgates have been well and truly opened, the river of tears, are making a nice neat puddle of wetness on my pillows and for once I just don't care. I don't move, not even to answer the phone or to eat, I just lay there until I have literally exhausted myself to the point where I have really cried myself to sleep.

A couple of hours later as I wake and struggle to open my eyes, due to the sleep that's in them keeping my eyes shut. I wonder what I have in to eat as my stomach is extremely unhappy with me and is expressing this, with an angry grumbling coming from that area. As I stretch my body out to its full length and sit up, the wires to my brain recall the memories of the day's events and I inwardly cringe. I don't know what was worse, finding out about the Carly and Jason's affair, or the awful way Carly tried to degrade me in front of everyone. Talk about smacking someone with a low blow like that. Obviously, I get she was trying to save face, especially being outed the way she was. Yes, maybe I never handled the situation in the correct manner. The grown-up and mature way to handle it, it should have been me probably asking to talk to Carly away from everyone, having it out privately woman to woman and maybe have either Pippa or Millie there to act as mediator. Hindsight is a powerful thing. It makes you think about what you should have said, but you didn't. How you should have acted differently, from the ways you did actually behave. However though, when you are there in the moment, all common sense and rational thinking goes out the window, because at the end of the day you are dealing with pure, raw emotions that come to the surface, and in some cases like myself, those emotions lead to a red mist descending onto you. You seem to act on impulse and all logic disappears. I am so grateful and glad that Harry acted as quickly as he did and stopped me from doing something to Carly, that for sure, I would later come to regret. Losing all control of my senses like that wouldn't have been the sensible option. Regardless of what the woman has done to me and the hurt she has caused, Carly didn't warrant that kind of behaviour. Violence is never the answer, no matter what has come to pass. As my mother use to say, 'Two wrongs don't make a right, Amber'. I quickly get my phone and send two messages the first one to Millie:

> Hi Millie, just wanted you to
> know that I'm okay. A little
> embarrassed, which I guess
> is understandable. I want to
> tell you how sorry I am, for
> spoiling the day that you had
> planned for us all to enjoy.
> I should and I could of
> handled it differently.
> Love you Lots xx

Once I have sent it, I think about what would be best to put in the next message to Harry. The best approach is to keep it nice and simple and straight to the point:

Hi Harry, just Amber here,
I want to say thanks for your
input earlier and your quick
reflexes. As I know I would
of regretted my behaviour.
Violence isn't the solution, I
know that. Cheers ears.
Take care
A x

Once I have sent that, happy that I put in a little humour into Harry's text, letting him know that actually I'm not angry with him or holding a grudge, for keeping quiet in regard to Jason's little secret. I leave my phone charging on my bedside cabinet and head downstairs as my stomach needs food urgently.

A few hours later, after a lovely chicken salad, a full bottle of wine and watching countless episodes of *Sex and the City*, I head back upstairs to take a shower. I need to wash away all of today's stresses and emotions. Yes, I may have lost a friend, but at least I have seen her true character and seen the real Carly. Frankly with the way that my life seems to be going in, there is no room for shallow, heartless and deceitful people in my life. Good riddance to bad rubbish if you ask me. Before going back downstairs, I grab my phone and see that there are a couple of messages waiting for my attention on my screen:

Don't worry about it hon, I'm
sorry that you didn't stay, but

we still had a good time over here. So nothing was spoiled really, the only thing that was missing was your presence. I totally understand why you wanted to leave though. Do you still want to meet up for brunch tomorrow morning? Let me know, speak soon and take care xxx

I quickly respond back telling her that under no circumstances would anything stop me from missing our annual brunch, and that I will meet her there at ten the following morning. The second message was from Harry saying:

Hey, don't worry about it. I simply didn't want to see you being carted of in a police car and being held in a cell. I think you've been through enough. I didn't realise how scrappy you can be. I kinda liked it, in a good sexy kind of way. If I'm honest I felt guilty being the one to have told you and all. Take care of yourself, Hot Stuff
H x

The last part makes me chuckle. It was nice to see a different side to Harry today, he very rarely allows anyone to see his compassionate, protective side. I am so used to seeing his cocky, jokey, fun-loving and flirty part of him. Which is always good to be around especially if you are needing a confidence boost. After today though it's nice to see that there is more to the bloke. I'm smiling to myself for some unknown strange reason as I head back downstairs to watch some more *Sex and the City* and pour myself another glass of wine. Knowing that if the alcohol is going to bless me with a humongous hangover in the morning, which is going to be extremely possible, with the consumption of alcohol that has been poured down my throat. Then the best hangover cure is at the ready, when I go to meet Millie at our favourite cafe, The Wide Awake café, for the biggest stomach-busting breakfast brunch you could eat. With that in mind the alcohol intake slows down a little as somehow I've already managed to put one bottle away and now a second one has been opened. My poor liver will not thank me for this kind of abuse, nor will my head in the morning. Then thoughts of Harry come flickering into my mind's eye, all six foot two of him. His light brown floppy hair, those baby blue eyes staring at me so intently that I suddenly become all hot and flustered and then that flirty grin of his, that is begging me to come to him. Wow, that positively proves I've drunken too much, which makes me instantly go into the kitchen, reach for another glass from the cupboard, fill it with ice from the freezer and water from the tap, then go back into the living room, lay on the sofa and continue watching my girlfriends from *Sex and the City*.

CHAPTER EIGHT

The following morning, as my eyes and body are starting to wake up, just as predicted those drummer boys are hammering away inside of my bloody head. Well, there is only one person to blame and that is my bloody self. As I literally have to drag my body out of the warm cocoon of my duvet and slowly make my way downstairs and head into the kitchen to fill the kettle up with water and have my morning coffee, which needs to be made extra strong to give me that additional kick I'm in dire need of, following that it's then time for the shower and try my utmost best to look half human and alive. I honestly thought, the amount of wine I consumed last night, would have knocked me out for the count, no such luck, though. I was awake most of the night, unable to switch my brain off. Yesterday's events repeated themselves over and over again, it was like my own mind wanted to continue torturing me. As I replay every little detail, the angrier and frustrated I was becoming again, which then led to me being extremely restless. After a horrendous night of tossing and turning and fighting with my duvet which seemed to last for a few hours, finally as night time was coming to its end and the start of a new dawn was about to make its appearance, did I then manage to get some shut-eye as the sun was starting to make his appearance. I don't know why but I've always thought of the sun as a happy, glowing, shiny male. I think the reason for that is down to a nursery rhyme I heard many a time when I was a little girl. My grandmother would sing it to me as she would sit me on her knee whilst putting on my shoes and socks, and rocking me at the same time, until finally the pair of us were ready to go and play at the park, when the sun was out. I'm sure it went something like:

The sun has got its hat on,
Hip, hip, hip, hooray,
The sun has got his hat on,
And he's coming out to play.

That's all of the song that my poor brain can really remember, in its hazy fog of memories when it comes to my grandmother and the fact due to my consuming hangover that will no doubt be having a huge impact on my memory also. I'm definitely sure there was more versus to the rhyme though. That little recollection has put a smile on my face, my grandmother died when I was a little girl. I couldn't have been older than four, maybe five. So as time is now passing on and the memories fade, so does the fact of trying to even remember what Grandma looked like and trying to recall the sound of her sweet singing voice. It gets harder all the time and the only thing to which I can possibly turn to now, is the few photos I hold of her and my mother, come to think of it.

So now, only when I conjure up the will power to look at my reflection in the mirror, does my attention take in the dark shadows under my eyes, which makes me look like a panda. Suffering now from a slight headache, from the combination of both the alcohol intake and the lack of sleep, my mood isn't much better either. So back in my bedroom, after my shower, on goes the music station with its eighty's classics, and other feel-good, cheesy pop music, while I get dressed and put on my make-up. Once all done and ready and I put the final finishing touches to my outfit, like the perfect jewellery, a little skinny belt and sprayed myself with my favourite Gucci Pink perfume. I am all ready and feeling uplifted to go out for my girly brunch.

It's another gorgeous day outside, the sun is glaring, its rays of heat and there isn't one cloud in the sky. The wind is blowing a gentle breeze and has that lovely summer warmth to it. You know the one I mean, it's as soon as the clocks go forward, the weather takes a pleasant change, you lose that iciness in the wind and just like that, overnight, the warmth and heat are making their presence known. I am one of those people who loves the sun, a typical sun worshipper, the hotter the better for me. When away abroad you can always guarantee where to find me, on a sun lounger beside the pool. Reading a good holiday girly summer romance book in one hand and a cocktail in the other. I go on holiday purely to relax and do nothing. Well, actually not nothing, as such, there are always some of the daily activities that the entertainment staff put on which I do partake in, such as French bowls, air rifle shooting, archery and water aerobics. Things like that, but the rest of the time, yeah, guaranteed you will always see me on the sun loungers soaking up the sun, and when I get a bit too warm, then in the pool I jump to cool down a little. Crap, now I've got holidays on the brain, it's making me want to look at a few places and maybe book somewhere, at least it will help me to be able to forget about my real-life problems for a couple of weeks. That actually sounds like a great plan and will probably bring it up with Millie and see if she fancies a girls' only holiday somewhere, it's been a while and we both still have some annual leave left at work. Cool, I am happy with myself and with that decided, it's put a bit of a bounce in my step and taken some of the edge away from my alcoholic-induced hangover.

Once I reach the Wide Awake Cafe, I notice that Millie is already inside sat at our usual table near the window. She looks up just as I'm about to approach the door and waves at me. Once inside the cafe and making my way straight to the table, Millie is looking at me with a stupid Cheshire cat grin on her face, it's that look that someone gives you when they know a secret or is up to something. That all knowing smug look, which can also be really annoying that you want to smack it of their mush.

"What's wrong with you? You look like the cat who got the cream," I say grinning down at her, as I place my bag under the table and take my seat opposite her.

"Oh nothing," Millie says with an irritating smirk.

"Well, that grin on your face says differently, come on tell me. Is there something on my face that has gone unnoticed or may have missed? I know that my dress isn't tucked into my underwear again. So come on, spill the beans."

"I want to, Amber, I really do honestly. On this occasion though, however much I'm dying to, well, a promise is a promise and unfortunately that being said I bloody can't say anything and it isn't my secret to tell. As much as my tongue wants to pour it out and it's so juicy, all I'm willing to say on the matter is that, it was something that Harry divulged to me last night. I'm not shocked though with what he said as the signs were all there, and to be fair, they are still clear to see. Anyway, that's for another day. Tell me how are you doing after yesterday, talk about me still being in total shock myself, so who knows how the hell you're feeling about the whole situation."

I don't actually say anything for a few seconds and instead look out of the widow and end up people watching, before bringing myself to do so. May as well be honest, no point in sugar-coating anything really, is there?

"All I'm saying is thank goodness and I'm ever so grateful to the person or the people who invented make-up, because today it's covering a multitude of blemishes and eyes that have huge bags underneath them. Thinking that drinking myself into an oblivion didn't do the trick either. As my head is causing me incredible pain this morning. Nothing that a big greasy breakfast cannot sort out though, eh?"

Millie has a chuckle at my little statement.

"Hear, hear, sister. I think most women around the world have thought or said the same thing at some point in their lives."

We sit in silence for a minute or two, whilst we both check out the menu before someone comes and takes our order. Millie goes for the eggs benedict and of course I opt for the classic stomach-bursting fry-up. I know whatever I don't manage to put away, Millie will no doubt finish it off. We both order two glasses of pure orange juice, followed by our usual coffees, for Millie she gets a cappuccino and for me it has to be my usual latte, the full fat one today instead of the regular skinny latte. I need as much fat and grease inside my body, to soak up all the alcohol that is remaining in my system.

Once our orders have been taken, Millie's phone goes off indicating a text message has come through. As she looks at who has texted her, she gives her head a tiny shake and quickly fires something back. The look on her face though says she wants nothing to do with whatever it is that is going on in her own personal life at the moment.

"Everything okay over there?"

"Yeah, it's just Sarah. Harry's ex. He is refusing to talk to her and he won't answer any of her calls. So she has got in touch with me to ask Harry to pick up the rest of his belongings."

Wow that has come out of nowhere, I muse to myself. I have to admit, though, the timing is a little suspicious. Firstly, Jason and I split up over a month ago, and now, Harry has finished his relationship with Sarah. Romance and cupid are really taking a hit at the moment. I feel as though Cupid needs to readjust his eyesight, or reanalyse the degrees and directions he is firing those arrows of his, because obviously his love matchings aren't cutting it.

"Crap, I knew that they had a bit of a falling out. I just presumed it was a lovers' tiff, nothing serious enough to end their relationship. Did he mention why? And is he okay?"

"All Harry said, is that he realised something that he thought that he had gotten over, but he said those feelings have come back to the service, that they never disappeared he just learnt to hide them and he doesn't want to brush them away again. He didn't want to string Sarah along and he knew deep down himself that it wouldn't go the distance. Harry couldn't do that to Sarah, she deserves better and as it has only been a couple of months into dating each other, no one really is going to be hurt. Whereas if he kept her there, giving Sarah the impression and hope that the relationship was moving forward, then that means more feelings and emotions are going to be invested more, and in the end, someone will definitely get hurt and that person would be Sarah. I'm just glad that Harry realised that now and actually thought with his head and not his dick."

Wow, yet again I'm surprised at Harry's behaviour, saying that though, that is Harry through and through. One thing you can guarantee in regard to the bloke is he knows how to treat and respect women. He hates to hurt anyone especially if that means letting someone down. The last thing he would ever want to do is to lead someone down the garden path, especially when he knows in his heart of hearts that there is no possible future there.

"You have a point with that last bit. Even so though, that is very mature of Harry as well. Thinking of someone else and putting that person before your own needs, shows how grown-up Harry really is and is also a very attractive quality in a man. Well, it is to me at least. It's nice to see that there is some decent, genuine men still out there, who have standards and good morals and know how to treat women right. Like you just said Millie, it's brains before penises."

Just as those last few words come out of my month the waiter at the exact same time delivers our food and Millie can't help but to grin. Her shoulders however start shaking up and down and I know that she is trying to control her outburst of laughter. Which in return makes me start to chuckle uncontrollably then proper laughter escapes from me. Doing my best to get myself under control, however I struggle as I've been hit by an avalanche of giggles. The poor waiter couldn't get away quick enough. Seeing his poor face turn from pasty white to a cherry tomato red and then as our laughter increased, he was a beetroot red by the time he could escape after placing our food and drinks down onto the table. Once the waiter disappears, does Millie let herself go. We end up getting stitches in our sides and we end up with the laughing tears. My stomach hurts so much that I end up having to hug it and beg Millie to stop, as it's her laughter that is increasing mine.

"Well, that couldn't have been timed any better now, could it."

"Trust you Amber, I haven't chuckled like that in such a long time."

Once we have managed to calm down and the giggles have subsided are we then able to compose ourselves, heck my insides are hurting so much it's as though I've done hundreds of stomach crunches. Grabbing hold of the napkin I wipe away the happy tears that are streaking my foundation on my face.

"Right anyway, going back to my earlier question, before yet again you cleverly changed track of conversation. How are you really feeling after yesterday and remember it's me you are talking to, so I know if you are trying to hide anything from me. Now go and don't hold back."

I sit there in silence for a few seconds, maybe a little longer contemplating on how to answer the question. Should I be brutally honest and put it all out there? Or should I skirt around the truth, with only a half of the truth, don't put all my vulnerable self on the table to be exposed. It's Millie though, my best friend in the world, if I cannot be truly honest with her then who can I be? And in the time we've known each other never have I held anything back from her before. However though, for the first time ever in our friendship, this time there is something holding me back and straight away my guard goes up. It has everything to do with Carly, as much as Millie mentioned yesterday that the two of them are no longer friends, I wouldn't want Millie to stop being mates with her, for one I'm not that kind of person and frankly neither do I want to put her in the middle of the two of us. These are my own personal issues with Carly, that will be and need to be dealt with but in their own time. If opening up to Millie and being honest with her, it's the worry of it simply getting back to Carly in any way. I'm not saying that Millie will do that to me, but as we know if there is alcohol involved, it can weaken your senses and all logic seems to go through the door. It's the fact that something could unintentionally slip without realising. To me it's a catch twenty-two situation, whatever way you look at it, it's a lose-lose situation for whoever is involved in this sorry sticky mess. At the end of the day though I haven't done anything wrong, why shouldn't I voice my opinions? It's me that's been hurt in the worst possible way, it has been my confidence that has taken a huge beating as well as my pride, it was me that was totally humiliated in front of all my friends. Why am I thinking of Carly? The simple answer is unfortunately I care and I know that Carly is a mixed-up girl.

"To be honest Mil, I'm not doing good at all. I know that I put on this persona that everything is good and life is fine and I'm over it, or I have it under control and moved on. It couldn't be more opposite though, these feelings are raw and fresh. The pain of betrayal is excruciating and overwhelming and I have this anger in the pit of my stomach that wants to let rip. Truly if Harry hadn't have held me back then I would have gone for her without thinking of the aftermath and more than likely would have differently woken up in the police cells this morning. I'm hurting a lot Millie and have so much anger inside of me and I'm not sure how to release it. What do I do? What would you do? To add insult to injury Carly and her vicious, nasty, vile tongue embarrassed me in front of all my friends like that, and talk about feeling ashamed of my own actions. I should have handled it all differently, Carly possibly reacted like that because of the way that I probably showed her up like I did in front of everyone. Talk about feeling so guilty for ruining the day. So yeah, that about sums it up really."

"Wow, fuck me Amber, that is a lot going on in your head and so many mixed emotions you are dealing with. One thing though, please if there is one thing that I can ask of you is to stop feeling guilty in regard to yesterday. The day wasn't spoiled, I've already told you that. We all had a good time still, minus your presence as after a few drinks you are the life and soul of the party. With the Carly situation do you think, maybe, you could ever meet up with her for a coffee and hash it all out? It may help you to move on and get some kind of closure. I could come with you and act like a mediator or you could take Pippa, she might actually be better in those kind of circumstances as she can be more impartial then probably I would."

"Not at this moment in time, Millie, sorry but I just can't. After I've got my head round everything and dealt with some of my own thoughts, maybe in a few months down the line, only then maybe, and that's a big maybe, will we be able to sit down and talk about it all. With the way things are at the moment and the raw feelings on both sides, I can't stand to see her face and no doubt she definitely won't want to see mine. I hope you can understand where this is coming from and the last thing I want is to make you choose sides or to put you in the middle of us. There is no reason why you cannot be friends with the pair of us, just don't have us in the same room at the exact same time."

"Yes totally, I get it and don't worry I know you wouldn't do that and if that was the case, there is no doubt whose side my hand would take Amber, you're like the sister from another mother I never had, you're like my sister and of course I will always have your back. Like you I've also be wondering and questioning Carly's loyalty, what she has done to you and carrying on being a good friend and a shoulder to cry on, all the while sleeping with your boyfriend is despicable. Who knows, maybe in time the two of you can come together and talk about it? You never know, you could be in a new relationship in a couple of months."

This makes me laugh. "Don't push it, Millie, my trust in lads at the moment is non-existent. Well apart from Harry of course and I'm not ready to jump back into that pond, just to invest my heart for it to end up being broken into smithereens, all over again."

"All I'm saying is, time is a great healer and you never know what is around the corner. Just don't shut yourself off completely, you may have already met the guy you are supposed to be with. The timing just has to be right."

"What? Like I should have got with Harry all those years ago before Jason came along, you mean?" I think back to that time. With Harry and I there is history between us, but we have always valued our friendship and we didn't want to ruin that. Yes, we have had a couple of drunken kisses here and there but it never went any further, even though we fancied each other. We had talked about it but both agreed that if the relationship never worked, could we really go back to being good friends.

It was a risk we both thought we could contemplate taking because we knew each other, we had the sexual chemistry, we made each other laugh and we had the banter in bucket loads. The number of times we have said that friends first make the best lovers and it is usually the relationships that start off as friends first are the ones that seem to last. So I just presumed that Harry would have acted on those feelings after that conversation, unfortunately though that didn't happen, because shortly after Jason came along and swept me off my feet. Then Harry backed right off and our friendship seemed to take a bit of a hit, especially when Jason was about. When my so-called ex-boyfriend wasn't present though, I saw a glimpse of the old Harry and his typical flirty ways towards me.

"At the risk of me repeating myself Amber, but we never really know what is around the corner, do we?"

We finish our meals and true to form I only manage a little under half of mine. Millie polishes off the rest as well as her own meal, like I thought she would. After the bill has been settled, we give each other a kiss and a hug goodbye. Millie goes her way and I walk towards the park, as I'm not ready to go back home on my lonesome, especially on such a glorious day. So before I go to the park, my path firstly takes me into my local Waterstone's bookstore where I pick out a good summer vibe novel that has some kind of romantic storyline to it. Yes okay, I'm still a romantic at heart and a sucker for love. You can't beat sitting in the park on a fabulous day like today and get lost in a bloody good book. That's what always got my attention and wanted to be when I was growing up, a writer and write books and become a published author. Well, it's only a dream of mine, I probably won't be any good at it to be honest, but hey who knows? Maybe one day. The reason nursing crossed my path was because of my mother as she was a nurse as was her mother, so it was expected that yes, I would follow suit, which I did to please my mum. It wasn't my dream job though, don't get me wrong at times the enjoyment is there regarding my job, but books and writing was my biggest passion. After I've made my purchase and make my way to the park, the perfect bench under a willow tree attracts my attention. It's the perfect place to settle for the afternoon, where I enjoy the peace and quiet, a little bit of solitude and soak up some of this wonderful sunshine. It literally looks like a perfect heavenly piece of garden paradise. The willow tree's branches hanging down and the leaves are gently flowing in the breeze. Remember those beads your grandparents may have had on the door frames and every time you walked through them, they made a gentle rattle sound? Well that's what the willow tree branches remind me of, but instead of beads you have the leaves rustling in the wind. The grass is a luscious deep green colour and scattered around are perfectly circular dug-out areas, which now hold some of the most beautiful and colourful flowers that give off the most pleasant of aromas. Like I said, a small bit of heavenly paradise.

CHAPTER NINE

A couple of nights later as promised, I'm in my kitchen cooking dinner for myself and Pippa. I'm doing one of my classics, a chicken pasta in a lovely creamy pesto sauce. To accompany it, I'm doing a simple but lovely garden salad with my own homemade salad dressing and some garlic bread, and to wash it down, I have cooling in the fridge a delectable bottle of a Pinot Grigio, which will go perfectly with our dinner. I have managed to cook the pasta, all ready to add the chicken, which is slowly cooking away in the oven before I break it up to add to the waiting pasta. The pesto and cream I will add a little later on as I don't want to over-heat the cream. All the components of our meal will come together, whilst the garlic bread is baking away in the oven.

I cannot lie, a part of me has been rather curious to find out what Pippa wants to talk through. It must be important as she never wanted to discuss it with anyone else around. I've noticed a bit of a change in her since she came back from visiting her sister, as long as everything is okay. I don't really know that much about Pippa's only sibling apart from that she lives in Hampshire on the Isle of Wight, which she moved to after meeting her late husband at an Isle of Wight festival many moons ago. Dawn is her name and she is the older sister by quite a few years. Oh, and she owns her own cafe called The

Beach Cove Café, on the beach front of Pebble Bank Bay. Pippa has offered me on many occasions to go on holiday down to the Isle of Wight and visit her sister and to stay in the holiday caravan that they both co-own, but unfortunately haven't ever really fancied it. I don't want to feel like I'm gate-crashing the party and invading Pippa's and Dawn's time together. Plus, it's one hell of a distance to travel to from Cumbria and with me suffering from the world's worst form of travel sickness really badly. Nevertheless, maybe one day. The pictures I've seen always look so beautiful, especially of the beaches and hearing that the lucky devils get around five hundred hours more sunshine than we do. It's a proper different kind of lifestyle down there, all of it is outdoor living and loads of beaches and water sports that you can partake in I believe. Also, they have a great cycling route which can take you along one of the best coastlines, well, if word of mouth is to be believed.

It's not the first time this week my mind has wondered, especially in the last few days, if Pippa is going to be packing up her northern roots and leaving the cold, grim, dark and dismal county of Cumbria behind, well minus the three good months we have, give or take a week or two. The winters here can be pretty bad at times though and Pippa isn't getting any younger. A change in climate, temperature and the better weather might just do her the world of good. If this was the case though, what would I do without her around. The selfish part of me would really not want her to leave. I've lost enough in the last month or two, my life cannot cope with losing anyone one else, especially Pippa, who has become a huge part of our small little group. We would all feel her absence in our own personal way. She really is that mother hen who has that typical overprotective maternal attitude, not in the bad sense though. Pippa worries about us, more so me and Millie, she loves to care and watch over us in that loving kind of way, where she means well. I trust Pippa more than anyone, if she sees that I'm going off in the wrong directions, she will gently coach me back to getting back onto the right path again. That's the kind of person she is and I adore her with all my heart.

Right on the dot of seven o'clock the doorbell goes and I hear the front door open and close, followed by Pippa shouting out, "It's only me pet."

"I'm in the kitchen, Pippa, come on through."

I give her a few seconds, to let her get settled and take her cardigan off before I pour her a glass of wine and put it on the table ready for her. Once the glass of wine is on the table for her, we embrace each other in a warm hug and straight away it feels like home where you don't want to leave or have the connections broken, before you know it though that warmth that was wrapped around you has gone and Pippa makes her way to the dining table to sit down so she can watch me at work.

"Dinner will only be about ten minutes," I say over my shoulder.

"Lovely, may I say it smells absolutely wonderful? My mouth started watering as I came through the door."

"Well let's hope it tastes as good as it smells then," I laugh back over my shoulder. Whilst I'm waiting on the garlic bread to cool a little before cutting it, I reach for my own glass and take a sip of wine and look over at Pippa and study her face. As I look at her properly for the first time in a while, there seems to be a few more wrinkles — or are they stress lines on her forehead and what appears to be dark circles under her eyes, forming as though she hasn't had a decent night's sleep in forever. This makes me increasingly worried and straight away I wonder if she has been suffering some health issues and kept it to herself. Maybe she doesn't want to worry the rest of us.

"Are you okay Pippa? You don't seem to be your usual self. What's been getting you all tense and before you say nothing, it's written all over your face."

I see her go slightly rigid before she relaxes again, with a smile that doesn't quite reach her eyes. This in itself is so unlike Pippa, for one there has never been any occasion where she's been uncomfortable about voicing her words, I turn my back on her, going about dishing up our meal. Just to give Pippa a minute or two to compose herself, without me glaring down on her. There was something I just saw, it was in her eyes, but for the life of me I couldn't put my finger on it. There is something bothering her, that much is as clear as the nose on her face, it's okay though, I can wait patiently until she is ready to tell me, in her own time. For now, at least, we are going to enjoy a lovely meal and have a good evening. Once the garlic bread is finally cool enough to cut, I put it all into the bread basket, the salad is all ready in the salad bowl with the dressing drizzled on top and the pasta dish is all mixed together. The food is all placed in the centre of the table so we can both help ourselves to whatever we want.

"Right, dinner's ready."

"Oh, this looks lovely, Amber, and it smells amazing, love."

We sit opposite each other in a pleasant silence and enjoy

a girly dinner, the realisation hits me that we haven't done this in such a while. That in an effect makes me feel rather guilty. I give myself a mental note to make more time for the dear woman who is sat in front of me. By heck she deserves it for everything that she has given to me. I could always cut down the hours at work and take her out more, then another thought enters my mind. The next time that Pippa mentions her holiday home down south and offers me the chance to spend some time down there as a girly holiday, then I will grab the chance with open arms. The last thing I want is any regrets and Pippa isn't getting any younger, an overwhelming sense of loss comes over me as I remember my mother and how quickly she was taken from me, and the things we never got around to doing. I don't want the same regrets with Pippa, no I must make more of an effort and make the most of the opportunities that come our way. As I know with my mother, once they have gone there is no way you can get those precious moments back, they are gone and gone forever.

CHAPTER TEN

Once we have finished our meal and the pots and pans have been scraped, rinsed and put into the dishwasher, we take our drinks into the lounge. I sit on my huge cuddle chair and let Pippa have the sofa, as she will be able to put her feet up and relax more. Unable to continue with the suspense of what Pippa is keen to talk about and obviously she isn't going to be the first one to broach the subject, so I think to give her a helping hand.

"So then, Pippa, I'm rather curious about what you need to talk to me about. Is everything okay? I mean really, okay? Is your health all right or has something been found? I've been sick with worry. You've been quiet most of the evening and I know something is bothering you. Whatever it is you can tell me and if I can help in any way then you know I will, or at least do my damn best to try. I'm sure it cannot be that bad Pippa, come on a problem shared and all that."

Pippa gives me a wary, watery smile. As though she isn't sure on how to broach the conversation. I notice that her eyes are becoming slightly moist. I quickly put my glass down onto the coffee table and go and sit beside her on the sofa and take her hand into mine, as the worry intensifies within me.

"Hey, what's going on, why are you getting so upset? You are starting to worry me now, Pippa. Please whatever it is, we will deal with it. I don't like to see you like this."

After what seemed like an eternity and thinking that Pippa was going to close up on me, she finally looks up and looks me in the eyes and goes to speak.

"I'm moving down south pet, my sister needs help running the cafe. As she is getting too old to do it all on her own now. Plus, I need to move away from here, the weather doesn't do these old bones of mine any good, especially in the cold damp weather, my bones are feeling it. I'm not enjoying life up here any more, Amber love, if truth be told. I want to enjoy the years that I have left. I don't enjoy the rat race any more and rushing around like a blue-arsed fly. I need to slow down, or else I'm going to be in that wooden box before my time is supposed to be up. Then I have to take into account all the travelling I'm doing going from one end of the country to the other, that in itself is physically draining especially for an older woman like myself, when you add the luggage and being on my own, it's so lonely. Moving down south, especially the Isle of Wight, well I'll be living the island lifestyle. It's a much slower pace of life, definitely warmer weather, and on the plus side, I get to help Dawn out, as she can take more of a back seat. You know me, I love being around people and meeting new faces and what a more perfect way to do that, than working on a beach-front cafe. Meeting new people and seeing new faces as well as the regulars that are very loyal to Dawn. It's what's going to make me extremely happy and what my life needs, now."

As I sit there and listen to Pippa, that overwhelming sense of emotions and the feelings of guilt swamp me and I feel so terrible that none of us hadn't picked up on how unhappy she has been recently. I guess I've been so self-absorbed in my own life and my own problems, that I haven't actually given a thought about what is going on in my friends' lives. Don't get me wrong I'm truly heartbroken and deeply saddened by this sudden news, as it was the one scenario my fingers were crossed for that wouldn't come about. Yet again my selfish thoughts think am going to be losing another person from my life? She is my surrogate mother and I need her desperately in my life, I honestly don't want Pippa to go anywhere. The sensible side of my brain knows though that she cannot stay here just for me and that isn't fair to Pippa, or to Dawn for that matter. I get a grip of myself and stop making it all about me, at the end of the day, if you love someone, then regardless of the situation you want them to be happy and didn't Pippa just literally say that this move will make her extremely happy? Her words not mine, of course. With that in mind then I too am happy for her and her happiness is all that matters, especially at this time in her life.

Pippa deserves happiness, she always does so much for other people, without wanting or asking for anything in return. The mother hen of our little group will be missed in so many ways and in so many lives.

"You need to do what is right for you Pippa. Every once in a while, you do need to stop putting others first and be a little selfish, in the good sense of the word.

"You need to at times bring your own needs and feelings to the front of the pack. I get it and totally understand why you need to go. Heck I'm really, really going to miss you though. When are you planning to go?" I ask her, keeping my composure intact as much as it's possible, considering the circumstances. I manage to get that little speech out before I start to crumble and end up crying once again.

"End of the month dear."

"Wow, that soon."

"That isn't all though, that is only part of what I have to tell you."

"Oh yeah, what more could there be? Let me guess, you've met a nice fancy man down there," I say as I wanted to put a little humour into the air, because things have just got that bit intense. We both have a little chuckle to that last part.

"Well, my dear, I was pretty much hoping and praying that you would come with me. Especially now after everything that has happened and with everything you've gone through, maybe a fresh start in a new place might just be the medicine to help you to move on. A new chapter, a blank sheet of paper, ready for you to restart."

I sit there in silence, in total shock and this change of direction the conversation has taken on, one minute I'm composing myself to the fact that I'm going to be losing this sweet lady, to life down south. Then bang, she hits me with another sucker punch and I'm at a loss for words.

"Wow, Pippa I really don't know what to say. I appreciate the offer, honestly, really I do. Heck, sorry I'm just in shock," I say as I get up from the sofa and start pacing up and down the living room floor, wrapping my arms around my body, taking it all in. I'm in deep thought, analysing the massive bombshell that Pippa has dumped, onto my living room floor. What the hell, is the only thing that is constantly and repeatedly, going around and around in my head. Unable to compute the information, my mind is in a daze, so to speak.

"Let me put this to you Amber, you know how small Carlisle is, whenever you go into town you are always guaranteed to bump into people you know. It is always the case and you cannot deny that. Now can you imagine at times, which it will definitely happen, you're in town and BANG. There you are standing in front of Jason and Lexi pregnant, glowing and looking beautiful. Then the next time which will happen, it's Jason, Lexi and baby. How will that always make you feel? I know you Amber, every time you see them, a little family. You'll be thinking to yourself that should be me, silently you will be hurting and being reminded of the pain, betrayal and hurt you've been through. There will be constant reminders that you can and never will escape from, no matter how hard you try. That's not what I want for you, baby girl. I want you to live the best life possible, and I honestly think that you could do that by moving away and starting a new life for yourself. You won't be on your own, you will have me and Dawn, who will love you just like I do."

I don't want to admit to it, however there is some truth to what Pippa has just said and I'm doing my best not to let the emotions get the better of me by chewing the inside of my cheek, which I didn't realise I was even doing until that awful metallic taste of blood presented itself on my tongue. I would in time though be able to get over it and the scars will not be as visible, that I'm pretty sure of. I'm more then sure that after the first initial time my path crosses with Jason's and Lexi's, yes it will hurt but that will get a lot easier with time, surely? Then the common sense takes over in regard to work, my home, my whole life here.

"It's not that simple though Pippa, I have my job, a career that's taken years for me to build, my friends, my life is here. I will know no one down there."

"Well not no one, you will know me and Dawn is very eager to get to know you." She sounds hurt that I have dismissed her and Dawn, in that comment of knowing no one.

"I'll be starting with nothing to my name, all over again. I'm sorry Pippa, but you are asking a lot of me. I'll be giving up everything I've worked hard for."

We both sit down and let the quietness grow between us, pondering on our own thoughts. Could I really pack up, sell my home and restart again, reinvent myself? The thought sends shivers down my spine and makes my terrified and scared, to the point where I'm becoming hot and clammy with anxiety. I have never been one of those impulsive people, I've always had a plan, a road map that me and my mother did together. To rip that up and destroy everything isn't me at all and what in heaven's name would my mother think, God rest her soul?

"Sorry Pippa, but I don't think I'm capable of doing that, I'm not as brave or as strong as you. If it was Millie, yes she would be long gone without even looking back, but me, I'm sorry, I haven't got the balls or the courage to pack up and move hundreds of miles away. Where I've no job, no home and I don't know a single soul down there."

"Amber at least spend some time to think about it. Give it a couple of days to sink in and please think long and hard about it, and if your response is still no, then I will completely understand and respect your answer. There is just a couple more things that might sway your decision or at least help you to decide. It is in regard to work and a place to live, you'll will be able to live in the apartment above the cafe, that would be yours and in respect to you working, well I thought you would like to work alongside me, in the cafe, you could work part time and the salary is good, Dawn likes to slightly overpay her staff. In your spare time what would really make me happy as well, I want you to take up writing again. You can really follow your heart and start putting pen to paper once more, write those novels you've been wanting to do since I've known you Amber. Just promise me please, that you will at least think about it."

Wow, Pippa has put a hell of a lot of thought into this and I don't know what to say now, as I'm sat there, listening to everything she is telling me. All I'm capable of doing and can do is bring my knees up to my chest and hug them tightly and let the tears run down my cheeks, because I'm hugely touched that she has thought of me in such a way and wants to do all she can to keep me close to her. Not just Pippa but Dawn as well extending such a huge generosity to someone she doesn't know, weakens my composure even more, if that is even possible. Pippa has not only provided me with a place to live and a job, but is also giving me the chance to follow my dreams, and what beautiful surroundings I will have to help me write. I am at a total loss for words, so I nod, get up from my chair and go and hug her tightly, letting her know that I will indeed give it a lot of thought. Once I know where my head is at, then, and only then will I let her know my decision and I know that there will be a lot of going back and forth. Not long after Pippa has left mine to go back to her place, I'm locking up, turning off the lights and heading upstairs to bed with a whirlwind of thoughts, ideas and emotions going around and round inside my brain, that I think tonight is going to be a night of more tossing and turning, because no way will I manage to shut down my brain, even if I wanted to. I am actually contemplating grabbing the bull by the horns and going for it, can you believe that? Because I sure can't. Moving to Pebble Bank Bay, on the Isle of Wight, Wow!

CHAPTER ELEVEN

A few days have now passed by since the mighty bombshell that Pippa dropped onto my living room floor. I have done nothing but go back and forth as I knew I would. My mind hasn't been on my job at all and to tell the truth the last couple of days, maybe even longer than that, my heart hasn't been in it either. I've been weighing up both the positives and the negatives in the two scenarios of leaving and staying. The positives obviously will be to get away from all the Jason and Lexi saga, that in itself is right at the top of the list. Other reasons for moving to pastures new, now include the weather, knowing that I will still be close to Pippa and where I'll be able to see her every day. It would be nice to relax more with a totally different pace of life, how did Pippa put it 'not rushing around like a blue-arsed fly' wasn't it? The piece de resistance, the golden nugget, to take up that pipe dream I had so long ago, to write. Right, the negative sides to that list. Well firstly, I would be leaving Millie and Harry, just the thought of that brings tears to my eyes. I cannot imagine them not being there in my life and seeing them at weekends. We have been in each other's pocket so to speak since we were young teenagers, I don't know if I'm ready to cut that umbilical cord with the pair of them, not yet anyway. Then I have proper job security that I have worked my damn arse off to achieve. Could I really throw all those years of blood, sweat and tears with all the difficult training courses down the drain? My lovely two-up, two-down home, that I feel in love with when I first went to view it all them years ago. There is a positive side to that though, I suppose I could put it up for sale or even rent it out, to a hard-working couple who will look after the property and love it as much I do. Like I've said, things have been going around in my poor head and it cannot seriously take much more, all the back and forth, changing my decision. I haven't spoken to anyone about what me and Pippa had discussed that night, not even Millie, my best friend. She is going to be pissed when she realises I've been sitting on this and keeping it to myself.

No, this decision is mine and mine alone. I cannot have anyone helping me or them having an input and putting in their two pennies worth, to which way I should lean. Which, if I talked to the others, they will surely have their own opinions and feelings on the matter and that isn't what I want. Seeing their anguished looks, and probably that sense of guilt, I know will be nestling nicely in the pit of my stomach. No, once my mind is made up and depending on my decision will I then tell people, well if that is the case. If the decision is to stay then no one need ever know. At the end of the day when all is said and done, I must do what is right for myself, especially when it comes to my own physical health and importantly my mental health and wellbeing. At this moment with the way work is going and the stress levels are incredibly high, that has made it to the negative side of the list and is pushing me towards leaving. That is not a sentence that I take lightly either. I'm feeling overworked, overtired and for sure is having a massive impact alone on my mental health. Just then a vision comes into my mind and it's as clear as day, I'm on the beach, sat on a lovely little beach blanket, a couple of towels are there beside me as though I'm not on my own, but I cannot make out the other person as it's a faded silhouette. However, we are laughing and so relaxed as we sit there taking in the views of the crystal-clear blue water of the sea, listening to the gentle waves lapping over the sand or stones. Literally, it sends a shiver down my spine as I come back to. It's like I'm getting an overwhelming pull from something to go for it. Heck, my mind is now playing tricks on me, yes, I'm definitely overworked and seeing things that obviously aren't there. The daydream seemed so bloody real, though.

That weekend I head into town to do some weekly chores, maybe a little window shopping and pick up a couple of holiday brochures from the travel agents before heading over to Millie's. As soon as I get off the bus, who do I bump into, but Harry. A little smile appears on my face thinking about the comment Pippa said only a few days ago and she is right, of course she's right. You cannot go anywhere in this town without seeing someone you know. I greet Harry like I greet all my friends with a hug and a kiss on the cheek.

"Long time, no see," I say cheekily to him.

"All right, Amber, fancy bumping into you. You going to be in town long?"

He is looking at me with that goofy grin of his that I'm so used to seeing, which brings me some comfort. That's the thing with Harry, he is so comfortable to be with and be around him, but there is also something a little different about him today, as well, it's the look in his eyes he's giving me. He is looking at me slightly differently today, than the rest of the times. The best way to describe it is seductive and intense, and to be honest, it's making me a little flustered and hot under the collar. A look of wanting, a look of longing. It is so fervent, that I need to look away quickly, before I melt to the ground into a pile of mush. So I look down at my feet and can feel the slight burn of redness coming to colour my cheeks. As I look back up at him again, in that spilt second the intensity has gone and looking back at me is the cheeky chappy, fun-loving Harry, with the mischievous twinkle in his eye.

"Erm... I need to do a few errands and pick up some brochures from the travel agents. So maybe an hour and a half. Then I'm heading up to Millie's."

"Cool, do you want to get the bus back together? I just need to do a couple more things, then I'm done."

"Sure, why not? First thing first though and that is a Starbucks. I always without fail need one of their coffees before anything gets done in town. Do you fancy joining me for one?"

"Yeah sure, you don't mind me tagging along?" Harry asks whilst throwing his arm around my shoulders and we comfortably walk side by side in perfect synchronisation and it feels as though our bodies are perfectly matched as we fit each other's curves, to perfection.

"Course not, otherwise I wouldn't have asked, you dingbat."

We walk to the coffee shop in a pleasant and comfortable silence. On the way, we pass the travel shop I wanted to go into. Breaking away from the warmth of Harry's embrace, I quickly run in, telling Harry that I'll only be a minute or two. There are so many brochures to choose from and without actually speaking to my best friend, I don't know whereabouts Millie wants to go on holiday, or where she is interested in going in the world — well apart from the fact it has to be an all-inclusive resort. So I pick a couple of brochures, one that has holidays in Europe, and the second is more long-haul luxury destinations. After saying thanks to the kind woman who gave me some advice on the better destinations, for two girls, who want some peace, quiet, solitude and tranquillity, I go to make my exit and leave the shop and smile towards where Harry is standing and waiting for me. However, I have noticed that his demeanour has changed and he is staring at something or someone. I reach him and follow his line of vision, the world stops spinning, I'm taken aback and the brochures that were in my hands only a second ago, have slipped from my grip and have landed on the ground. Harry is now aware of my presence, he quickly picks the brochures up from the floor, and tries to drag me away from the scene that is in front of me.

"Come on Amber, ignore it and let's just go."

I can't move. My legs and feet have been weighed down with cement, I'm getting a fistful of knots in my stomach and feel my eyes welling up. There they are, the two of them across from me at the nearby jewellery store three shops away from the travel agents, is Jason with who it looks like a very pregnant Lexi and what looks like to be ring shopping. They look so happy and smile adoringly at each other. Jason has his arm around Lexi's waist and lovingly strokes her baby stomach. Whilst Lexi has her arm around Jason and snuggles closely into the pit of Jason's arm. Just like I use to do only a matter of months ago, the grief and sense of loss is all too consuming. Even after this much time why does it still hurt? Why are the feelings so raw? I honestly thought it wouldn't affect me in such a way, obviously I was wrong.

Before I can get my composure together and get my arse away from there, they both look up and Jason must have sensed someone looking at them, because he slowly glances towards the two of us, just at the exact same time as Harry puts a protective arm around my shoulders. The evil stare that Jason gives to Harry is so uncomfortable, his eyes are simply boring into Harry's, it's a look I've never seen before from Jason. He is looking at Harry in an incredibly harsh way, and this makes me intensely nervous. At that moment amongst all the other emotions I'm feeling, I have enough time to think boy, what's his problem? Why is it we are getting the filthy looks? He's the one that did the dirty. What in the name of heaven gives him the right to look at us with such nastiness as though we betrayed him? He whispers something into Lexi's ear and they both then look over at us, then she looks back at Jason, grins to him and they both head into the shop. Talk about a Cheshire cat grin that Lexi purposely just gave to me, said it all really, he's my man now, I've got his baby growing inside me and I'll have the ring on my finger. I've got further with him, than you ever did. I'm grateful to have Harry's arm around to keep me standing and supported, otherwise I really do feel as though I would be in a heap on the ground.

I tell Harry I'm not in the mood any more for that coffee and that my errands can wait till another day, the wind has literally been taken out of my sails. I just want to get away from the town, away from Jason and his pregnant girlfriend, who I guess is going to be more than his girlfriend pretty soon and will become his fiancée by what we've just witnessed. Pippa's words from a few nights ago are repeating themselves around and around in my head and are indeed ringing so very true. She is so intuitive and has a massive insight to this kind of thing, it makes me wonder has her life course taken her onto a similar, if not the same path as mine? Has Pippa been so in love and something so drastic happened to her, that she remained single because the pain was too intense that there was no way in hell that she was going to put herself through the suffering again? Is that what she meant when she gave me that little speech in regard to love, to be open to it and not to shut myself off, because love is the biggest gift in life.

Am I always going to feel like this and more importantly will my body always freeze on the spot as I have just done at the sight of them both? Another thing that Pippa was definitely correct about, was, as much as I hate to admit it, I do actually think to myself — that should be me going ring shopping, that should be me carrying his baby, why isn't it me? Do I also not deserve to have that same kind of happiness, what makes Lexi different to me? What has she got that I haven't? What was it exactly about me, that didn't warrant such a committed commitment from Jason? All that self-doubt is coming to the surface and I cannot control all the negative thoughts that are coming to mind. I honestly thought to myself, in the five years that we were together, that was the route we were heading down. Even through all the troubles we had at times and even towards the end with all the arguments, I really did think we would see it through all those rough patches and make it to the other side. Just like all other couples and what their relationships go through, what doesn't break you will only make you stronger and bring you closer together. In Jason's case however instead of putting in the effort to make the relationship work, he was putting in the effort elsewhere for a better relationship following his wandering eye. What is that saying again — *they think the grass looks greener on the other side*. Well, until that goes south and they finally realise exactly what they had and what they've lost. Whether this will be the case for Jason I don't know, however I sincerely hope not for the sake of Lexi and that little bundle of innocence that they are bringing into the world.

As me and Harry reach the bus station, I hand him the brochures to take back home to Millie.

"I'm really not in the mood now, can you give Millie my apologies and I'll give her a ring later tonight. I just need to be on my own at the moment."

"Yeah, no worries, are you sure though Amber? Having your friends around you right now may just do you the world of good and it will help to occupy your mind away from certain things. Being on your own, your mind will be fixed on the one thing you don't need to be thinking about and that could be pretty depressing Amber, you really don't want to be going down that road. Come on, let us help you we're your friends, we are all here for you, please remember that."

"Thanks Harry, that's is so sweet of you to say and I'll keep it in mind but, at this precise moment, I wouldn't be very good company at all."

I give him a big hug and for a second or two I don't want to come out of his embrace, as I feel so safe and warm as though there is a shield of protection around me. I quickly step away from him and give myself a mental shake, one thing's for sure, I cannot be moaning for one guy and enjoying being in the arms of another. My emotions are so messed up, I give him a weak wave goodbye, then turn and walk away doing my best to hide my confusion of mixed emotions.

CHAPTER TWELVE

As I get myself seated on the bus, I'm sitting next to the window and just look out of it and go far, far, away, into my own private mental daydream. Where life should be much simpler and far happier, but not in my case as my daydream is full of complex questions and my thought process takes its own journey. I have so much to think about and I don't have the answers, well I don't think I do at least. Why is it when it comes to life-changing choices for you to decide, your heart is telling you one thing and your head is saying another? Which one do you trust and which one do you listen to?

Your heart is all full of emotions and feelings, by listening to your heart you will end up following your emotional inclinations, as I have learned in the past. Whereas if you heed what your head is saying, it is very possible it may come up with numerous, different and quite logical reasons why you should act as it is advising. However, the downside I guess is it can make you at times second guess yourself a lot and you don't want to be doing that either, that I do know because it is something that I specialise in, as I'm commonly known for doing that exact thing, always second guessing myself. So I suppose the most sensible conclusion I can do for me is to take my time, make no rash decisions and weigh up all the factors and possible outcomes. At the end of the day any emotions whether good or bad can cloud my judgement and influence my decision. So the sensible approach would be to listen to a little bit of logic and listen and trust my heart, only then will I have made the best life decision purely for myself.

Right, knowing that I really need to put that into practice in regard to packing up and leaving. Leaving my home, leaving my friends, all in all leaving my whole entire life and what I know behind. With fresh starts come, new beginnings and a clean chapter, because right now the way I'm feeling, running away seems like such a good idea. If I don't take this fantastic opportunity that Pippa is handing me on a plate, no doubt I'll come to regret it sometime in the future. Then there's my conflicting and mixed emotions which are totally freaking me out in respect to Harry. Actually, putting distance between the two of us might just help me, then at least I will know if those feelings are real or not. The last thing I want to do is treat Harry as a rebound to make me feel better about myself, give me that boost in confidence of still being wanted by a guy. That isn't fair to anyone and the potential damage it could have on mine and Millie's friendship, that in itself isn't worth thinking of. As that friendship means the world to me, and something I treasure and wouldn't want to jeopardise in the slightest.

I get off the bus three stops before my own and walk to Pippa's. Now knowing which way I'm leaning for sure, and in my heart, I know I've made the right decision for myself. I just hope that what I've decided pleases Pippa and puts a smile on her face. Once I reach her door and after knocking, I wait patiently, whilst I'm waiting for some unknown reason, I start to go all clammy and nervous, but with my mind made up I will not allow the nerves to win and get a hold of me. Not this time, no thank you.

"Amber, darling, what a pleasant surprise. Come in, come in. Can I get you a drink or anything, tea, coffee, a gin?"

"A coffee would be lovely, thanks Pippa," I smile back and say in response.

I go and sit in her sitting room and wait patiently until Pippa comes in with a food tray full of goodies from biscuits to cakes and two large mugs of coffee. I opt for one of my all-time favourites and a good old classic of a French fancy to have with my drink. I love coming round to Pippa's as the whole environment of her place is so cosy and has that proper homely feel to it, it does feel like I've come home. It makes me think of my mother and how much I really miss her.

"You were right Pippa."

"Right about what pet?"

"I've just come from town and bumped into Harry and we thought we'd go for a coffee. Well, to be honest it was me that suggested it. Before we did though I had to quickly pop into one of the shops and as I came out, there was Jason and Lexi a few shops down and they were ring shopping."

"Ah, I see. Oh, sweetheart, please don't start crying, you have wasted enough tears on that boy."

"But you were right as much as my brain hates to admit it, all I could think of was, that should be me. Five years of my life invested into something that wasn't actually going anywhere, that's five years I will and can never get back."

Pippa says nothing, she just quietly gets up and sits next to me, takes me into her arms and gently rocks me back and forth.

"Will it always hurt this badly, Pippa?"

"No love, not forever, they do say that time is a great healer. It may not seem like it now, but this pain and hurt that you are feeling is raw but it will subside and one day you will wake up and won't be feeling it any more and you will finally move on with your life. Unfortunately, though, there is no timescale of how long it will last, it all depends on the individual. It is from heartache like this that we can learn from and it can also help us to grow."

I let what Pippa just said to me sink in, wondering if time really is a great healer, or will a small part of me carry a small piece of this hurt around as a reminder to never let anyone get close to me and letting them in, ever again.

"Your true love is out there somewhere Amber, and like yourself, he is trying to find you and get to you as soon as he can. It may take a while but he will get here, that I'm certain of. It may not be tomorrow, or next week, or even next month, but I do promise you he is getting here as quickly as he possibly can. You just need to be a little patient and to remember when it does happen, which it will, to make sure to let your guard down and let them in. Open your heart because, when you do sweetheart, the gift of love is the richest and most blessed gift, in the whole, entire world."

"You are such a romanticist aren't you, Pippa," I say with a small giggle. "And yes, I know you're right, but I'm not too sure if I believe in all that soulmate crap."

"That's because you haven't found the right man, yet." Pippa interrupts me by saying.

"What I do need to do though is to focus on myself for a while and find out who I am again, because I seem to have forgotten. I have followed other people's life choices that have been laid out for me and I have continued to trail along those paths without any grudges and without moaning, because I knew that people especially my mother had my best interests at heart. Now though I need to do what is right and best for me. So if that offer is still open Pippa, then I would love to come to the Isle of Wight with you. There is a *but* though, before you say anything. I thought I would see how it goes for the first six months, and if it all goes well and I enjoy it down there, then I'll make the move more permanent."

I have never seen Pippa so happy and I'm extremely overjoyed that she has excepted my compromise. I have listened to both my head and my heart, but at the end of the day I'm going to follow my heart with a little logic from my brain. I can always sublet my house out for the six months, as much as I like nursing, my heart isn't in it any more. It is time now for me to follow my own path in life and stop living it for other people. Pippa is so excited that she is talking ten to the dozen, talking about the places we can visit and the day outings we can take. Pippa's enthusiasm is so contiguous that for the first time in a long time, I too, am excited for this new chapter in my life to begin and to see where it will take me. Wow, could a proud northern girl like myself, become a southern belle? I do like the accent and hope that I can pick it up a little, it might just give my harsh accent that little bit of softness to it. Secondly though what I'm really looking forward to the most is putting pen to paper again and writing, maybe I will be able to write my first book. Something that really burns like a passion within me, and I love and do truly miss.

After another hour or so at Pippa's I finally take my leave, not before however we put arrangements into place to meet up next weekend to discuss when to leave, decide on a time and date. The discussions of which ferry to get and which ferry company will be the cheapest and which port to go from. When Pippa travels down there she usually goes to Southampton then gets the single foot passage ferry over to the Isle of Wight. As long as we have a plan of action then I'll be happy, old ways are hard to let go I still like to have plans mapped out, everything else I'm more than sure, will fall into place.

We say our goodbyes and with a spring in my step I happily walk home, as it's only a fifteen-minute walk. The only part of my plan I'm not actually looking forward to is telling Millie my news. The number of scenarios that go through my mind is unbelievable, the one that I'm hoping for though is that Millie is supportive and happy for me and can understand why I'm doing this. I suppose there's no time like the present to start putting the wheels into motion. I reach into my bag and grab my phone to call her and notice that I have two missed calls from the woman in question.

"Amber thank goodness, I've been trying to call you."

"Yeah, sorry Millie. I've been over at Pippa's and my phone is still on silent. Just noticed your missed calls now."

"Oh right, you should've come round to mine," she says, sounding a little hurt.

"I know I could have, but I really needed to talk to Pippa about something."

I now realise, that I can't really tell her my news over the phone, this was actual face-to-face news. Plus, would it make me a bit of a chicken doing it over the phone, because if it got difficult or extremely intense either one of us could hang up on the other and that is one scenario I certainly don't want to happen.

"Anyway, you're not at work tomorrow, are you?" I go on to ask her.

"No, I'm not back in till Tuesday."

"Cool, how about I pop over say around twelve and probably bring a bottle of wine with me?"

"Okay, look forward to it. How are you doing anyway Amber? Harry told me about what happened in town earlier. I'm so sorry you had to see that, especially it being so soon after the break-up. I am so grateful though that you weren't on your own."

"I'm okay now thanks. I've received one of Pippa's lovely, sweet pep talks. Right now though, I'm walking home, looking forward to having a long soak in the bath, a luxury face mask, then order a takeaway and maybe watch a movie."

"Okay then hon, as long as you're sure you're okay. Well, enjoy your evening and I guess I'll see you tomorrow and we can have a proper catch-up."

When I get home, I don't even bother with the bath or the face mask, instead opting for a quick shower, get into some comfy loungewear, order myself my usual Chinese takeaway meal. All the while having loads of adventurous thoughts going through my mind, now with my decision made all that's left for me to do, is to enjoy the ride and another thing, for the first time in a long, long time, I'm actually feeling the excitement within me to write again. I can literally see myself on the beach, people watching and putting pen to paper. I can do this, deep down I know I can. Finally realising that I'm no longer scared of starting over again, I put on my trusted friends from *Sex and the City*. Now this is the blissful way to spend my Saturday evening, the only thing missing is a gin cocktail which I can easily forego.

CHAPTER THIRTEEN

I'm here in Millie's kitchen with a lovely cool glass of chilled white wine in my hand and enjoying the aroma coming from the lunch that my dear friend is making for me. From the looks of things and from what I can smell, I'm going to be plated-up a fabulous seafood pasta dish with a green side salad to accompany it. Millie has cooked this meal once before and it was simply delicious, I can feel my month watering as I personally wait patiently until the pair of us can tuck in and fill our stomachs with such splendid food.

"Harry not about today?" I ask as I haven't seen him loitering around the place, usually he would be sprawled out on the sofa remote in hand and speed flicking through the television channels. What is it they call it, telly serving or something along those lines?

"Football match, think he said. He is part of some five-a-side team. Then him and a few of the lads are meeting for a pint or two afterwards."

Well, that's good to know I think to myself, it will be bad enough to inform Millie about what planned actions I have in store for myself. I'm simply grateful not to be having Harry putting in his two pennies worth as well. At least this way Millie can tell him later on once the bombshell has been dropped and I've left and probably without a shadow of a doubt have a bit of a gossip between the two of them, and more than likely think I'm being extremely foolish and acting irrationally by letting a man drive me out of town. I know they will both have their own opinions on the matter of why I'm leaving, but as much as they may hate the idea, they need to remember that I'm doing this for me and for me alone and that for once to get on board and be very excited about the prospect of a possible new life that's waiting for me, out there.

I'm sat at the dining table and my stomach is ready to burst, I'm that full I could quite easily lay on Millie's sofa and have myself a leisurely afternoon nap. The seafood was completely amazing, a mixture of mussels, king prawns, salmon, clams and tuna and complimented the sauce Millie used beautifully. All sat on a bed of tagliatelle pasta. Her side dish of green salad, which consisted of lamb's lettuce, spinach, watercress and rocket drizzled over with a lemon dressing and fresh herbs finished it off perfectly.

"Wow Millie, you've really outdone yourself. That was so tasty and delicious, I'm fit to burst."

I can't move at the moment, we are just sat at the table chatting about anything and everything most of it rubbish, as well as drinking down the lovely bottle of white she had to complement the meal and the flavours. After fifteen minutes or so once my stomach has settled a little, I push myself up from the table and gather the dirty plates. The least I can do is the washing up after such a sumptuous meal was prepared for me.

"So then," Millie says as she looks up at me from where she is sitting, giving me such an intense stare that I turn my back to her and start filling the bowl up with hot soapy water to make a start on the washing-up. "Do you want to talk about yesterday?"

"What about yesterday?" I respond back over my shoulder without looking at her.

"Well, the fact being, you saw your ex-boyfriend supposedly ring shopping with his new girlfriend, who he cheated on you with and got her pregnant all behind your back. I don't want to add insult to injury or anything Amber, honestly I don't, but it must have had a massive impact on you."

"What do you expect me say, Millie?"

"How about the truth? Be honest for once, Amber, let it out. It's just you and me."

"Well, the horrible truth of the matter was, it was simply awful. It felt like I was being pierced in both my gut and my heart all over again by the sharpest of knives possible. To see it and be witness to their happiness made me ill. My feet felt like they were being cemented to the ground, so no matter how hard I tried, I couldn't actually move. All the while I was screaming to myself internally asking myself, why wasn't that me? It hurt so bloody much to see how blissfully happy they both were, to the point where I could have quite easily gone straight over to them and punched the happiness off his proud gorgeous face and let him see my hurt and my pain, to let him see what he had done to me," I throw back angrily. I've stopped doing the washing-up at this moment and dry my hands on a tea towel. After drying my hands, I rest them on the worktop and lower my head, doing my best to take in deep breaths after my outburst. Letting my shoulders drown a fraction, as the stress and anxiety slowly does its best, to leave my body.

I stop what I'm doing, because if I carry on, no doubt I'll end up breaking something and probably end up cutting myself with broken glass or a sharp knife because the pathetic part of me can't pay attention to what I'm supposed to be concentrating on. Why does everyone want me to open up and talk all the time? Why do we always have to come back to the topic of Jason and Lexi? My friends are supposed to take my mind off the matter and cheer me up, aren't they? They know how much I'm flipping hurting, please just let me deal with things in my own way and time, let me talk when I feel ready and actually want to talk honestly. Do they not realise, that by always talking about it, they are making it worse for me? Don't get me wrong, I know that sometimes talking can get things off your chest and I get that, my friends are only worried and concerned about me. Nevertheless, by getting me to talk about the same shit over and over again, is in fact having the opposite effect and for some reason they cannot seem to grasp that concept. I do try and see it from their point of view and think to myself, if the boot was on the other foot what would my own reactions been like, especially if someone treated Millie the way I've been treated, the answer is the same. I would want to get them to talk too, this once again makes me feel so guilty for being snappy to my friend, when all she wants to do is be there for me because she cares.

"I'm sorry Millie," I say turning round to face her. "It's just that I spent most of yesterday talking about the same crap with Pippa. I just haven't got the energy to go through it all again."

"I was just concerned about you Amber that's all, but I understand it can be quite tiring talking about the same thing all the time, too. So why don't we change the subject and talk about something more joyful, shall we?"

Just like that all is well and like any true best friend Millie knows what to say and what to do. I give her a huge grin, put the tea towel back onto the side and go and give her a massive cuddle. The tension in the air that was there a few seconds ago has disappeared and in its place are two girls being silly and laughing. Once we have the washing-up completed and the kitchen is looking all clean and spotless, Millie makes us both a coffee and we go and relax in her lounge. Where she does her usual thing of putting the music channel on low on the television so we have a little background music. I wait a few minutes whilst we both settle, before I broach the subject of my intended and upcoming decision to be moving away. I grab the bull by horns and delve right in.

"There is something I do want to share with you, Millie, actually. However, I'm going to be honest, you may not like what I need to tell you though."

"Well, this sounds intriguing, to say the least."

"Shit, this is harder than I honestly thought it would be."

"Just spit it out, Amber, for the life of me, I cannot imagine it being as bad as your making out."

"Well, the thing is, I'm moving away. I am going to move down south with Pippa. Six months at first, and if things work out, and obviously I end up liking it down there, and all goes to plan then I will be making the move down south permanent."

All Millie can do is look at me in that gormless fashion, mouth open and appearing speechless, mimicking a goldfish perfectly well.

"Wow, that's a bombshell and a half, and I for one, was

definitely not expecting that at all. Heck, I think something a lot stronger than this coffee is very much needed."

Millie takes herself into the kitchen, probably to get a grip and to compose herself. In the meantime, I'm left here with my own thoughts, whilst waiting patiently for her to return to the lounge, I know that I had better prepare myself for the interrogation she is going to hit me with, and the possibility that she'll be throwing a lot of questions towards me. I do my best to picture myself in her shoes, and once again, for the second time today, wonder what my own reactions would be towards Millie. Well for starters I would have acted the exact same way, first I would be rendered speechless, then no doubt the shock would consume me, before probably finding myself begging her not to go and lastly cry and admit how brave and courageous she's being and wish her all the luck in the world. So knowing that those would be my reactions, this puts me in a better position for what to expect from Millie, as in a way we are kind of two peas in a pod and think very similarly to each other. Most importantly I would spend as much time as is humanly possible with her, before she departs for pastures unknown.

I wait patiently for what seems like an eternity, before she wanders back in with a tray. On it is four glasses all together two wine glasses and two shot glasses with what looks like tequila in them, with a side dish of salt and lime wedges. As Millie puts the tray down onto the coffee table, she asks for my hand to put some salt on, passes me a shot of tequila and places the wedge of lime in front of me.

"Bottoms up," Millie says as she clips my glass and in

unison, we both lick the salt, and shoot back the tequila, which burns the back of my throat, and I quickly reach for the lime piece to suck on it, so that it can take the taste of the bitter liquor away.

"So then, when was all this planned?"

"You know when Pippa came over for dinner last week?" All Millie does is give a little nod of her head, so I continue. "Well, she explained about her sister, how she is getting older and not getting any younger and is now finding it quite difficult doing a lot of the heavy work herself. To cut a long story short Pippa is moving to be there for her and to work alongside Dawn in the cafe, and she asked me to go with her. I could work part-time in the cafe, I would have the two-bedroom apartment above the place, and in my spare time as Pippa put it, I can do what I once upon a time loved to do and that is to write again." A few minutes of silence follows, once I have finished talking, and as I watch Millie's reaction, I do my upmost, not to grin or giggle at her.

I can see the cogs going round and around in her head thinking of what to say and each time she thinks of something, she goes to open her mouth to say it, but stops as it seems another thought has just popped into her mind. She literally reminds me of a goldfish, you know when you watch them in their tanks going around opening and closing their mouths with only air bubbles being released? It's not the first time that she appears to be at a loss for words. I cannot keep it in any longer as a small giggle escapes from me, there is only one thing for me to say to break the silence.

"Cat got your tongue over there? You simply look like a fish instead of words coming out of that open and closing mouth of yours, it appears only air has escaped."

Hearing the sound of my voice, brings her back to the here and now, and finally, starts speaking.

"Is this because of Jason? Because if that's the only reason, Amber, that sadness, that pain, the anger you are feeling as well as the bitterness you are experiencing it will in time all but disappear. I know you're heartbroken, Amber, and I get it, you know I do. I've been there, remember, when me and Tom suddenly broke up a couple of years back, but to literally run away and worse still letting him drive you away, it is completely bonkers."

I let her get her rant over and done with without interrupting her once. All I can do is just sit there and listen to what she has to say and you can hear the sadness in her voice and the upset as though she is confused with the decision I've made.

I realise that I need her to understand that finally this isn't about bloody Jason, Carly, Lexi or the baby any more. Actually, it's about finding me again, who am I as a person and who I want to be in the future. Also, that age-old question that you always get asked when you are younger, what do I want to be when I'm all grown up? I know that most sound silly to a lot of grown-up people, but fortunately for many they knew what they wanted to be from a certain age and they pushed forward and mapped out their plans with the help and loving support from their parents and finally, in time and hard work, they have achieved their goals. Others like myself live their lives through their parents' choices. In my opinion that is extremely selfish of parents, as they have already lived their lives, they shouldn't try to re-live them again through the lives of their children.

"Millie, I need you to understand that for once in my life, I'm going to be doing something for myself. Yes, that may seem selfish to some. This isn't about anyone else any more, but solely about me and what I need in regard to my own personal issues."

"But… but."

"No Millie, there are no buts. I need to rediscover myself again and Pippa has offered me a fantastic opportunity to do just that, and I would be foolish to at least not try. I intend to grab it with both hands, I don't want to have any regrets with the choices that are offered to me. I want to get that passion back into my life, something I truly love doing and seeing my hard work come together with the finished product. Something to be proud of."

"But you can write here, Amber, you don't have to move hundreds of miles away to start writing again, surely."

"Millie, I really need you to hear me, listen to what I'm actually saying, please. I have collected a lot of bad memories that I no longer want to be around, and I would love it if you can get on board. I want a fresh start, a new beginning filled with lots of happy memories. This is really scary for me too and it would be lovely to have my best friend beside me, getting on board and supporting me one hundred per cent."

I'm mentally exhausted and all talked out, I'm an emotional mess. We both sit staring at one another, as we both let our feelings show and allow them to come to the surface and we let the tears trickle down our faces. Crikey, this has been an emotional roller coaster of a day.

"Oh, come here," Millie says, leaping up from her chair,

to come over to me and folds her arms around me and I do the same to her. I hold onto her so tightly as I'm aware that in a matter of weeks I won't be able to do this any longer and that in itself makes me depressed and sad.

"I'm going to bloody miss you, Amber."

"Ditto. But we can still talk face to face over FaceTime or Messenger." I pull myself away from her and look her squarely in the eyes and say, "I will miss you too, Millie."

We sit back from each other, dry away our tears and we do that typical girly smile where it says a multitude of things, but to us it says all is going to be okay and that we're good.

I was about to broach the subject of our girly holiday aboard and an idea that came to mind, instead of actually travelling far and wide, why doesn't she come down south and have a traditional English stay-cation instead? Before the subject could be brought up however, the sound of Harry at the front door entering his key into the lock puts a stop to that topic of conversation, obviously this is signalling the arrival of Harry's return home. So I take this as my cue to start making tracks and let Millie fill him in, in her own time.

"Not going on my account are you Amber?" he says, as he enters in that typical goofy way of his, that always makes me smile. Man, damn that twenty-watt smile of his and for a split second or two it stops me in my stride, I quickly pull myself together thinking how incredibly stupid I'm being. I really can't be coping with this right now, it is purely loneliness that's making me feel a pull towards Harry, heck I'm not even attracted to him in that way, am I? NO, NO, NO. That has to be it, I'm feeling lonely and all my emotions are heightened at this moment.

"No, I'm just feeling tired and to be honest I am bloody drained of all energy. Nothing that a long soak in the bath cannot handle. I will give you a call later tonight Millie," I say as I go and give her a kiss on the cheek and head to her door to leave.

"Don't I at least get a hug too?" Harry asks as he partly blocks my path. I look up at him and smile, damn him for looking at me in that sultry kind of manner and his eyes boring into mine. Is it me or is that a look of lust I see as his pupils dilate and it makes me receive a butterfly fluttery feeling in the pit of my stomach? Shit, how can I refuse him a hug? We embrace each other and once again I get such a warm and comfortable feeling of wanting to stay in the fold of his arms. The smell of his cologne is intoxicating on his neck, that my downstairs area seems to be wakening and paying attention. That pull of sexual chemistry is stronger than last time, and it scares the crap out of me, I don't need this now especially not now, not with me moving away. I quickly jump back as though I've been burnt, resulting in me dropping my bag to the floor. Quickly I pick it up, say my goodbyes and take my leave, not before though, I see the small look of hurt on Harry's face.

CHAPTER FOURTEEN

I cannot say that the last three weeks or so haven't been incredibly busy for me, because if I did, I would be lying to myself. I have literally been non-stop doing my best to get everything all tied up. Tonight, though I can finally relax and enjoy the evening that has been planned out, as tonight Millie has thrown me and Pippa a leaving party and it is going to be the best Friday night out ever, Millie's words not mine. Pippa and I are leaving early Sunday morning. The company that has been arranged to move all our belongings, well they are sending out their removal van out tomorrow afternoon. There was no point in me hiring out my own moving van, as I came to the conclusion that renting my place out fully furnished made more sense. All I'm taking with me, are some personal keepsakes that I cannot part with, obviously my clothes and footwear that's a given, all my books, CDs and DVDs, to be fair I haven't got that much in respect to the CDs and DVDs. The heavy load is mainly all my books, there are so many of them, that somehow, they need to be reduced and the ones that don't make the cut, will be going to the charity shop. Some ornaments are coming too, and not forgetting my happy memories and that is my photos through the years. Anything else that's needed I can always purchase once I'm down there and settled. The apartment that will very soon become my new home comes furnished itself with all the mod cons. So the six or seven boxes that have been filled and packed, taped and written on so I know what's in each one and some I've marked extremely heavy, so the moving guys know to be careful when lifting them. They will quite easily fit in the back of the moving van with Pippa's belongings.

It didn't take long to be honest to box up my life's possessions, it was quite sad really you would have thought over time one would have collected more than what I had. However though, I am giving a few items away to a housing charity. Millie came to give me a hand at the start of the week, sorting through all my clothes and splitting them into three piles, one pile would be for the items that would be going with me, the second pile would be for the bin, and the third pile and not the least, would be items of clothing and footwear that would be sent to the charity shop or in Millie case what she wanted to keep for herself. It was quite emotional really, but also, as I was going through my things and looking at some old photos from the past, I realised to myself that not only am I moving, but my life here was coming to the end of an era. That in itself is extremely sad, amazing isn't it how you can pack up your complete life in boxes and that's it, your existence no longer belongs here. On the flipside though I will have exciting times ahead of me to come, yes, the unknown is a little scary, however I suppose that's what's going to make my new adventure fun. Here I am more than willing to welcome in the new era of my life with no regrets.

As well as packing up my place, I have also managed to get a new tenant to rent my house and they are moving in on Monday. They've agreed to renting the place over the next six months with a view that it could be extended if they were interested at a later date, depending of course on my own circumstances and how things go for me. I was pleasantly surprised how quickly the estate agents had managed to find me a tenant so speedily to be honest, saying that though I do think that for my lovely two-bedroom property they are getting it slightly under the normal rental asking prices for the area. Well, I didn't want to appear overly greedy, as I was practically moving into a place rent free. One good turn deserves another and all that. The last thing I need is karma giving me another kick in the stomach.

In regard to work, I've been asked on a couple of occasions if there was any way I would reconsider and stay on by my ward sister, but as much as once upon a time I did love my job in the beginning and I truly did, nursing really wasn't what and thought it would be in the end. I really did honestly think to myself that I'd get to know my patients as individuals and spend time with each and every one of them. To care and to be there for them in their time of need. Not to spend most of my time sat on my arse behind the nurses' station, filling in countless amounts of flipping paperwork. Towards the end I was glad to hand in my two weeks' notice and finished my final night shift yesterday morning. I was awarded for all my hard work with countless amount of good luck cards, a bottle of white wine and a bottle of gin as well as a huge bouquet of flowers. In the staff room there was a leaving cake and balloons, saying *Bon Voyage*. The cake didn't stretch far and some staff missed out, which wasn't pleasant as people missed out on the lovely moist chocolatey sponge, with a velvety chocolate ganache and the sweetest of vanilla buttercream. It was like having the smallest of food orgasms in your mouth. That was such a nice surprise and not one I was expecting in the slightest.

It was a weird feeling as I walked away from my colleagues, and the ward I have worked on for the last so many years (I think it's been about five years I've worked on EAU) for the last time yesterday. As I was leaving the hospital for the very last time never to return here again, (well here's hoping, fingers crossed) an overwhelming sense of sadness came over me and from nowhere the feeling of tears started escaping from my eyes and trailing down my cheeks. For the life of me though, I couldn't understand why this huge feeling and being incredibly upset came from. Was my sub-conscience, trying to tell me something that I hadn't considered? Or was it that I actually felt a huge amount of guilt knowing that if my mother was still here, then I was letting her down and giving up on the career she wanted for me? I gave myself a little shake and a small pep talk. Surely though she wouldn't have wanted to see me miserable, in a job that no longer brought me any enjoyment or where I wasn't happy any more? Nursing was a little different in her day, I've heard the stories from the older nurses that had also worked alongside my mother who themselves are due to leave to enjoy their retirements. I am quite positive that my mother would have wanted to have seen her only daughter doing something that she loved, wouldn't she?

I hear the sound of a horn outside my house, so I go and quickly have a look outside my bedroom window, just to double check that it is my taxi and not some other neighbour's relative. Sure enough, though, and bang on time for a change, it is my taxi. The driver presses his horn for a second time, showing me of his impatience at having to wait a minute or two. I quickly pick up my bag from my bed, double-checking that I have everything, lipstick check, money check, bank card check, mobile got it. I give myself one more glance in my mirror and head out to my waiting ride.

"Where to?"

"Da Vinci's please," I answer him politely back. I will not allow his rude bluntness to annoy me which in turn will have an effect on my mood. All I will say on the matter is, what happened to, *Hello, where to then, love*? Manners cost nothing you know. I honestly think that peoples' manners are going further and further down the drain, what's unacceptable is that it gets worse with every generation. No, I refuse to allow it to annoy me any further, I sit back, rest my head on the headrest, close my eyes and take a few deep breaths.

As we drive to my all-time favourite Italian restaurant, I'm glancing out of my window, and as silly as it may sound to some people, I am giving certain places my own personal goodbyes in my head, obviously. Don't want people thinking that I'm some kind of nutcase going crazy and need to be admitted to hospital. I am to be fair quite sentimental that way. Some of these places hold such great fondness and treasured memories of time gone by for me. Especially once I turned eighteen, wow me and Millie have had some crazy wild nights out here, and come to think of it, Harry has with us to. Once upon a time it used to be the three of us, the three musketeers painting the town red. A small smile starts to spread across my face as I have a memory or two come flashing back to me. A few times on some of those nights out me and Harry shared a few drunken kisses here and there at the end of a night out. At the time as I recall my motto was, a good night out was a success if it meant that you finished the night of with a kiss from a handsome stranger that you met and found attractive. When on a couple of occasions this didn't happen then Harry was always there, more than willing to oblige, he didn't mind at all. Well, I didn't think he did, and to be fair to the bloke, Harry, even to this day, has and always was the best drunken kiss I've ever had. Wow, weird isn't it how suddenly some flashbacks just enter your mind from absolutely nowhere? Or why they were triggered in the first place.

Talking of Harry actually, I don't really think that he has taken the news of me moving away, too well. He showed up late last night, seeming extremely drunk and smelling like he had drunk a liquor factory completely dry. He was doing his best to talk to me, bless him. However, what he was saying didn't make any sense whatsoever he was just slurring so damn much and most of it sounded like complete and utter gobbledegook. All I could got from him and could understand was a lot of *why's, love, us*, and oh yeah, the word *bastard* was repeated quite a lot. Then suddenly he went quiet and was doing his best to stare at me like he was trying to focus intently, then his hands were on either side of my face and he was staring deeply into my eyes, well as much as the drink would allow him to. As he was pulling me in closer to his face, and just as his lips were about to touch mine, he made this horrible throaty noise and quickly let go of me, and turned his back and just in time reached my grass and was sick on my lawn. How romantic eh, NOT. Honestly, I was embarrassed for him, he was repeating his apologises over and over and all I did, because I was so annoyed with him, was tell him to go home and to sleep his drunkenness off and would talk to him at my leaving do tomorrow night. I watched him leave once he was out of sight, I then quickly went into my kitchen and filled up my washing bowl and went as quickly as one could back outside with it and threw the water onto the grass and tried to wash as much of the sick away as I humanly could and try to get rid of the awful smell of it. Man, it was so gross, it was that intense the smell that it nearly made me hurl myself. Once I'd finished doing that, on impulse I grabbed my phone, and sent Millie a quick-fire text:

Just to give you the heads up
your lovely drunken cousin is
absolutely hammered and kindly
left me a present on my lawn,
a nice pool of vomit. I've sent him
back to you, so you may need a
bucket for him, or get him to sleep
next to the toilet. See you
tomorrow night. xxx

I didn't hear back from her, she was worse than me when it came to being houseproud. Whether or not Harry will be here, or show up at all tonight, especially after last night, then that would be anyone's guess, you just don't know. I guess we will see soon enough, won't we?

I am hoping that Millie hasn't gone overboard with the party planning, I didn't want anything big or elaborate. It would be nice just to have a very small personal group of close friends no more the six and then afterwards we can finish the evening with a few cocktails and a good boogie somewhere. Maybe, just maybe, for old times' sake and one for the road, I could bring that old motto of mine, back for one night only. A drunken kiss at the end of the night with a handsome attractive stranger to finish my evening, my last night out in town back in my single days ending on a high. That man in question was Harry. With a cheeky wiggle of his eyebrows, at the end of the night, and his mischievous smile, knowing neither one of us had pulled. He would pull me into his arms, and plant his lips on mine. It was so sweet and nice. Even in those drunken kisses, you could feel the chemistry. At that last little thought I have a tiny chuckle to myself just as we are pulling up outside the restaurant. Wondering if I could possibly get a repeat of that kiss, from many years ago. Or will that involve me stepping into dangerous territory? No, I'm not going to overthink anything, I'll just see where the night leads to.

CHAPTER FIFTEEN

I pay the taxi driver my fare with a small tip which he more than likely doesn't deserve, but I've always believed in being polite, I open my door and get out of the cab. Once I've stepped outside, making sure that my dress is all straightened before heading inside and making my big entrance. I absolutely adore this dress I've chosen to wear tonight. It's a strapless black just below the knee-length pencil dress and it hugs my skin and curves perfectly, the top part of the dress has this amazing green pattern intricately sewn on, which gives it that little bit more off that vava-voom. As I'm approaching the main door however, there's this silhouette figure there standing in the shadows outside the door that I haven't seen in a while. Oh, you have got to be freaking shitting me right now, I don't need this especially not tonight. Why or why pick this night of all bloody nights? Man, she has a flipping nerve, I'm thinking to myself. I know that she can hear me approaching her my heels aren't exactly quiet, as the sound coming from them is like a horse walking along, going clip clop, clip clop. As she turns towards me it's like all of a sudden, the world is moving in slow motion. Fuck, do I really have to deal with this right now, right here? Man, talk about wanting to behave like a typical toddler who throws a tantrum and stomps their foot in frustration because things don't go their way and saying repeatedly no, no, no, no, tonight is all about me. I cannot really see any other way out of this, talk about having to be the bigger person here and stand my ground and get this over and done with. It's not like there is any bloody chance of avoiding her and enter the building via another door, and this is the only way in and out. I'm sure climbing the back fence dressed like I am to enter through the kitchen door at the back of the building is totally out of the question. Put it this way, if that was at all possible in the slightest, I would about turn and use it.

"What the hell are you doing here, Carly? I'm pretty sure that you weren't invited, you better not have been."

There is nothing from her to start with, she seems as uncomfortable as do I and that's saying something, especially when it concerns my ex-friend standing across from me. Carly has always been one of those girls who oozes confidence, but at times that over-confidence she has can cross the line and can make her come across as being extremely arrogant and cocky in fact, which in turn can piss a lot of people off, more so women. So to see her standing in front of me moving uncomfortably from one foot to the other and appearing to be at a loss for words, takes me by surprise and I'm quite taken back by it. There is something else that's different, too. Her hair is unkept, her skin appears to be oily and greasy and the weight seems to have dropped from her, like she hasn't eaten a decent meal in a while. I'm stunned to say the least, what the hell has happened to the look she prided herself on? It's like the former girl I once knew has disappeared and in her place is this shadow of her former self. To the eye if you didn't know her as well as I do, you would think she was some kind of druggy. That sounds horrible I know but I don't know how better to describe her appearance.

The silence starts to stretch a little too long, until the atmosphere is starting to feel a little uncomfortable. I simply haven't got the time for this crap. I start to walk past her towards the door, when suddenly the feel of her hand is on my arm, and she grabs me to stop me in my tracks.

"Amber, I'm truly and utterly sorry for what my actions did to you. Above all else I really need you to believe that. At the time, yes, I was incredibly drunk and obviously wasn't thinking of anyone else but myself, and what I wanted. That isn't an excuse, that I acknowledge. I was selfish and thoughtless and was just hoping that with time you will be able to forgive me and we can move forward."

"It doesn't really matter now though does it, Carly? Because at the end of the day the damage has been done. You put shagging another woman's bloke first, to make it worse, your supposedly best friend's bloke, need I add, before your friendship. Where was your loyalty, your integrity? Have you never heard of girl code? You simply take what you want when you want without a shadow of a thought and don't ever think of the consequence of your actions, Carly, and look where it gets you."

"I know and you're right, all I can keep saying is that I'm really sorry," Carly repeats as she starts to cry. For once I'm not seeing the crocodile tears either, that this woman is so good at putting on, and an act, I, like others, are so used to seeing. Yet, she is proper sobbing big teardrops, and her shoulders are going. It's plain to see that what she is saying, is actually coming across as meaningful. This becomes quite awkward for me now, as I find myself in a catch twenty-two situation. As one part of me, the quite angry side, still thinks, well, she has made her bed now she needs to lay in it, she has brought it all onto herself and she only has herself to blame at the end of the day. However, the kinder, more forgiving side of me, just wants to go and give her a hug and tell her that maybe, in time, we can start to build bridges.

Carly at times can be her own worst enemy, with certain decisions she chooses and the actions she takes. Which she does under the influence of drink and I'm sure that at certain times there have been drugs involved. Don't get me wrong that doesn't excuse her behaviour in any way and I would never accept that as a reason for her behaviour. She makes all these choices and they are bad ones at that, without a thought or a care for anyone else's feelings and she really doesn't think of the consequences her own actions have on other people and the lives she could potentially destroy. It does make me wonder how many men has she been with that are in a relationship, engaged or even married. She really is a law unto herself and the worrying thing is, if she continues going down this path of hers the way she's going, she is going to end up being one hell of a sad, lonely old woman, with no one in her life.

You know what though? I'm tired of it all. I'm leaving in a day or so and there shouldn't be any bitter feelings left behind, I want to leave here peacefully. I don't want to start my new life with this hanging over me, I don't want any form of baggage following me or any hatred, because at the end of the day that will only be hurting me in the end. So there is only one way to handle this and do what's right for me in this situation, Carly has made the first step and any fool can see that she is deeply remorseful.

"Come here," I say to her as I approach to go and give her a hug, no longer wanting to hold a grudge.

"Everything isn't as it was before, it will take time and patience on both sides, Carly, I'd need you to understand that, Okay? In the meantime, though, let's start with building up the trust and taking it one step at a time. How does that sound?"

"I get that, and it's better than I could have possibly asked of you, in all fairness."

"Okay, thanks for understanding. Anyway, one thought has been on my mind, how did you know that we would be here tonight?"

"I saw Millie in town the other day and she mentioned about you all having a get-together here tonight. Then she went on to say that if I wanted to clear the air, then this would be my only opportunity to do so. So that explains the reason why I've shown up unannounced, clearly not wanting to go inside and appear that I was gate crashing or something."

The door to the restaurant suddenly opens with such force, that it literally makes me and Carly jump out of our skins. As I check to see that the door is still attached to its hinges, there standing in the doorway are Millie and Pippa, they are both staring straight at the two of us. Pippa, bless her, is looking between the two of us with such a stern look that it reminds me of a school headmistress, who knows what's going through that sweet mind of hers. Then she looks at me and the look turns from stern to worried, like she wants to know if I'm okay. Millie on the other hand however is looking a bit taken aback, man she would make a great actress, she must have expected Carly to show up to some degree, as she put the damn idea into her head. She looks so comical at the same time. As she has a cig hanging out of her mouth whilst it's being held between her teeth. I should put them both out of their misery really and inform them that all is all right, especially Pippa.

"Don't worry guys, everything is okay, we've talked and all I will say is, all's well that ends well. Do you want to come in Carly and have a drink with us as it is mine and Pippa's leaving party? Not to be rude or anything but it looks like you could do with a bloody good meal in that skinny arse body of yours, you look like crap. Afterwards, if you're interested, we will be going to a club for a few cocktails and dancing. So if you want to join us then the offer is there."

"I'm sure we can ask the waiter if he could set another place setting at the table," Millie responds, looking relieved that her plan hadn't backed-fired on her. Talk about taking a risk, the cunning little minx. As I finally head inside, I notice that Pippa is still giving Carly that stern glare and not moving from where she is standing. I wonder what could she possibly want, or be thinking for that matter.

"Pippa it's all sorted now, please, are you coming back in?" I say.

"I'll be in in a minute love. I just want a private word with Carly for a moment. Go on, you and Millie head back inside."

"Okay, but this is your party too, Pippa."

"I know dear, it will only take a minute, that's a promise."

Millie foregoes her cigarette and grabs my arm and we both head inside to the rest of our party. All the while I'm thinking to myself what is going on, what has Pippa got to say to Carly that she can't say in front of me? Don't get me started on the stony look, that Pippa was giving to the girl either, yes okay, everyone knows Pippa is protective over me and likes to be that motherly figure and maybe that's all it is. Nevertheless, the look that passed between them said something completely different and there is some underlining issue, that has escaped my knowledge obviously. For tonight though I'm going to drop it, for once I'm going to let it go over my head, refuse to get involved and have a bloody good evening. I mean, nothing can go wrong this evening to spoil my last ever night out in my home town can there? Everything that could possibly happen has already transpired and shown its ugly head. No, tonight is going to go off without any more hiccups. Quoting what the pop/rock artist Pink would say, "Let's get this party started, because people are waiting on my arrival."

CHAPTER SIXTEEN

Once Millie has managed to drag me inside, well at least halfway inside the restaurant. She abruptly stops the two of us and looks at me.

"You're not mad are you, Amber?"

"Well, I won't lie to you, Millie, it wasn't what I was expecting to see when my arse got out of the taxi, that's for sure. I was shocked to say the least, and that soon turned to anger at the sight of her standing there, waiting for my arrival. You do realise, that potentially, you could have ruined my night, not just my night, but Pippa's as well? Who knows what is going on out there, and what is being said."

"I'm sorry, Amber, I wasn't thinking. At the time it just seemed that it could be a good time for you both to talk and clear the air, and maybe bury the hatchet before you left on Sunday. You've been friends for too long, I just thought, oh who bloody knows what I thought, to be honest. Maybe the hope that you both could possibly put the past behind you and probably move forward. To be fair to me though, when I did mention it to Carly, well frankly I did actually think that she would be a no show. After all, its Carly, but obviously after seeing her show up like she has done, it really goes to show how deeply sorry she must be and that in itself is a rarity for the girl."

I ponder on what Millie has just said and as much as I

would hate to agree with the sly minx that she is, my best friend does have a good point. For Carly to apologise for any of her actions, is unheard of, maybe, just maybe, this could be the turning point of changing her personality just that little bit.

"Come here," I say to her with a smile on my face and opening my arms out to her to give her a hug. "All I will say on the matter is, it's a good job that your cunning little plan worked out."

"Cunning… What me…? Never."

We both start laughing as we make our way to the table that's been reserved for our group, where we will be spending the next couple of hours, eating, drinking and simply having fun.

There, at the table waiting for us, are two of my closest work colleagues, Gina and Chrissy. Then, to my surprise, I see Harry sat there looking a little bit sheepish, he looks at me with his cheeky little grin and I just give him a smile and a small wave back. Next to him is one of his mates Joe, who I haven't actually seen since the incident of the BBQ at Millie's. I make my way round, giving everyone my usual hugs and cheek kisses and thanking them all for coming tonight.

Then I hear the angry words being spat out of Harry's mouth.

"What in the name of hell is she doing here, who would even dare invite her?"

"Harry," I warn. "Please just keep quiet for me, if not for me then for Pippa."

"But I don't understand what she is doing here, Amber, man she has some audacity to just show up."

"Listen, I invited her in to join us, she was waiting for me outside, with compliments of your cousin. We talked and to put it mildly I'm tired of it all, I'm leaving in a day, so what does it really matter? Let's just move forward, Harry, please. Now, promise me you'll keep a lid on it, at least for tonight, or till I've gone okay?"

Harry doesn't say anything, instead he asks the passing waiter if he can have another drink and he just sits there distant, quiet and moody. It's impossible to help myself as I walk up behind where he is now sitting and wrap my arms around his shoulders and hug him tightly, kissing him on the cheek and whispering softly in his ear 'thanks'. Unfortunately, I get nothing back from him. Fine, if he wants to act like a petulant child, who has been scolded by their parent then let him. I refuse to let him or anyone, ruin my mood or my night.

Once we are all finally seated at our table including Carly, the waiter comes and takes our food orders and we also go and order three bottles of wine for the table, two white and one red, as well as a couple of bottles of sparkling water. The atmosphere becomes full of light-hearted banter and loud laughter and everyone seems to be getting on great. Pippa is in her element with Harry's flirty talk, and a couple of times I see her flick his arm, in a fun-loving way. She loves it really, as it keeps her young, and it makes her feel youthful. Pippa and I, catch each other's eye, and we give each other a big grin and a cheeky wink and give our glasses the smallest of raises to privately toast the pair of us, and I know that she is all okay, after the talk with Carly. I see that Chrissy is flirting with Joe, who I may say looks slightly uncomfortable, but is taking it in his stride. Millie starts to fill everyone's wine glasses and stands to make a small speech. She goes on to say all the usual things that people say in a farewell speech, a lot of we wish you luck, how much you'll be missed, may your new lives be filled with happiness. Then before you know it the rest of the group raise their glasses to toast me and Pippa and to new beginnings.

"Oh, and just one little thing. I forgot to mention, I may just be following you both down there."

I look at her in total shock. Wow, would my best friend really move all the way down south? I know that she is coming down in about a month's time or so after I have settled into my new place. We thought it would be a good idea for her to come to me for a holiday, once I manage to find the right time to putting it across to her, and we were both in agreement instead of us both going aboard this year, she would come to me and enjoy the finest that England had to offer for a stay-cation.

"Really?" is all I'm capable of saying.

"Yes really, after Pippa and I talked about a week and a half ago." Millie stops talking at this point as I look over to where Pippa was sitting. She has the biggest grin on her face, then she looks back at Millie, giving her the nod to carry on.

"Well, me and Pippa have been talking a huge amount recently, the conclusion we've come up with is, I can get a feel for the place when I come down at the end of September, and see what I think of the place. Pippa then mentioned that maybe you would like to have a roommate and I could possibly work in the cafe part-time as well. Then Pippa gave me the killer offering, that as we know some of the places here in town are closing because of the ridiculous London price rents on the properties and gigs are too hard to come by, as the pubs and clubs already have their own regular singers, well I could take up my singing again living down south. Apparently in the high

151

season down there, the pubs or bars and all the holiday places, are wanting good singers. I could try and get a gig at least two nights a week. What do you think?"

I simply have no words. All that seems to be happening is the happy tears escaping from my eyes, I stand up and head over to Millie and pull her towards Pippa, who stands and the three of us are all hugging, and I'm crying and laughing at the same time, along with my, and yes Millie's, surrogate mother and my sister from another mister. Wow, the secretive little minxes, planning this behind my back has to be one of the best gifts ever. Pippa never seems to stop amazing me, with her thoughtfulness, kindness and generosity. Talk about being one in a million.

"Thank you, Pippa, but what about Dawn? Is this okay with your sister?"

"Of course, it is. On a Friday evening as Millie put it, we can have an open mic night at the cafe. She is going to take control of it, and there are a few more great ideas that she has floating around in that pretty head of hers. It'll be good to get new younger ideas to get the younger crowd into the place."

Wow this really is a fresh start for the three of us, and from fresh starts, come new beginnings.

After what was such a lovely meal and some bloody great news and good conversation, we all leave the restaurant and start to head for our favourite club called Storm to do some dancing to burn off some of the calories we have consumed. Well, all of us apart from Pippa. Millie and I walked her to the taxi rank and again I couldn't stop thanking her for the opportunity that not only was she giving me but also to Millie. Pippa was really one of those people who were one in a million. Once we had hugged her and said goodbye and after quickly telling her that I would be ringing her in the morning and then saw her safely into a cab. Me and Millie walked to the club to meet up with the rest of our party, who were waiting outside the club, for us. Once inside the place the lads go and get the drinks in, whilst us girls go and try to find a table. Luckily for us a booth opened up as the previous occupants were just getting up precisely as we were passing and Gina was quick to ask if they were leaving. It was one of those large semi-circular booths that can seat up to six people with a couple of extra chairs at the end of the table. I love it here, Storm holds a lot of happy memories from the past gone by. The DJ is playing some classic eighties tunes at the moment, and there are a few on the dance floor dancing away to the tune I now recognised as Rick Astley's *Never gonna give you up*. The dancers are singing out loud, badly if I may add the chorus to the song. The atmosphere is so upbeat that it's contagious, I end up dancing at our table, while Gina and Millie sing out the words. The floor feels sticky under my feet indicating that alcohol has been spilt onto it some point through the evening, and whoever has tried to clean it hasn't done a very good job, as the sugar from the drink has created a gluey adhesive, form now.

Harry and Joe come back to the table with a large pitcher of lager, a bottle of Prosecco and two Cosmopolitan cocktails, obviously they were both for me and Millie of course, how well Harry knows us. The tunes were banging, everyone was having a good time and starting to feel mellow with the consumption of alcohol that we all seemed to be putting away. Harry reaches over to me and takes my hand into his and gives it the smallest and gentlest of squeezes, followed by soothing strokes with his thumb, then leans over wanting to speak. Luckily, we are sitting next to each other which makes this easier, I lean my head closer to his and he speaks into my ear and apologises for his behaviour last night. However, I'm unable to concentrate properly on what he is actually saying to me, as I'm finding myself becoming aroused by having the touch of his lips so close to my ear and feeling the warmth of his breath on my skin. It is such an erotic feeling that I don't know what to do with myself. All I'm able to do is quickly reassure him that no harm was done, because if I stay this close to him for much longer, I won't be accountable for my actions of saddling myself over his lap, running my fingers through his hair, whilst gently pulling him close enough to touch lips that will lead into a deep steamy kiss. Knowing this, I must distract myself so quickly I get up and grab Millie, asking her to come and dance with me and pull her towards the dance floor.

Wow, alcohol has definitely heightened my womanly senses, the tingling sensations that was coming from downstairs was unreal or something has happened to wake up my womanhood and that something is Harry. My next drink needs to be water, or at least a soft drink. I cannot continue drinking alcohol if my body is betraying me like this. Just then the DJ plays one of mine, Millie's and Carly's favourite tunes, *We are Young* by the very cool American band I know to be called Fun. Carly is straight away making her way to join me and Millie on the dance floor, and as the chorus kicks in, the three of us are drunkenly bad singers, and start to shout out very loudly the words *we are young and we will be setting the world alight and on fire*, not giving a care to the world because in that moment at that time, it is just the three of us and no one, and nothing else exists. I am having such a fabulous time and I'm so grateful the night has taken the course it has done, I feel like I'm becoming more myself and how I used to be once a upon a time, many, many, moons ago. A couple of lads seemed to have gravitated towards where we are and have joined us on the dance floor. Where they came from I don't know and frankly don't care, it just feels nice to receive some male attention. It does wonders for the female ego and it gives me a confidence boost, so with the small group that we were, and now a little bigger, we start to form our own little dance circle. The blokes make us laugh at their moves that is obvious to them, thinking that they are good dancers, which in fact are really bad dad dancing moves. One of them asked for Millie's number which she refused to give out, after that they seemed to move on to the next group of girls on the dance floor.

After what feels like an hour's worth of dancing, Millie, Carly and myself make our way through the mass of dancers and leave the dance area and go back to our table. As we make our way through the throngs of crowded people, making sure we don't knock anyone's drinks and approach our table, straight away my attention is diverted to see that there are a couple of girls and one of them is sat on Harry's knee, not saddling him like I wanted to. No, she is sat across his lap and has her legs crossed with her arm casually wrapped around his neck and they seem to be deep in conversation. The sight of this sends the ugly green-eyed monster to rear its unattractive head. Then all of a sudden, the girl (who I'm ashamed to say it I am giving daggers to) she cocks her head back and lets out one of those deep, dirty laughs. I cannot understand why, but I get an overwhelming attack of jealousy. When we arrive at the table, I don't bother speaking to them, instead I just reach for my drink, noticing and thinking that Millie has clicked on to my hostility. Once my drink is in my hand I down the lot of it, making out that the dancing has made me hot and thirsty. Which is a very plausible excuse, as the clear beads of sweat are running down my face for everyone to see.

"Who are your friends?" I hear Millie say. As I do my best to appear nonchalant and pay them very little attention, childish yes maybe. Yet my alcohol-induced brain finds this quite hard to do, because through my peripheral vision I can see the leggy blonde stroking the back of Harry's head and running her fingers through his hair. All the while I'm thinking and wishing that, that was me, instead of her. I start to imagine what it would be like to be sat there, just like she is and have the feel of Harry's touch on me. The feel of his arm wrapped around my waist and his hand resting just above the cheeks of my buttocks. Turning my face into his and letting our lips lightly touch each other's. Inhaling that intoxicating cologne of his, that drives me crazy. I give myself a mental shake, what the hell am I playing at? I cannot possibly be falling for Harry, can I? Those feelings I presumed where long gone, but have I only buried them and now they are making their presence known once more. I need air, as my lungs feel constricted and I can't breathe.

"Does anyone want to go out for a cig?" I say loudly. I don't even bother to wait for anyone to respond, as I grab my bag and literally speed-walk out of the place.

Once outside, the feel of the crisp cool night air soothes me. I find it so refreshing after being in a packed-out crowded building, absorbing everyone else's body heat. I put my back against the wall and slide down into the crouching position and put my head between my knees. I greedily take in a couple of deep gulps of fresh air. Once my lungs have taken their fill, do I then force my brain to start concentrating on slowing and calming my breathing down to normal. Shit, what was that? Some kind of panic attack?

Then I hear the sound of Gina's voice. "Amber, me and Chrissy are going to start heading back to our place, we're both shattered, and unfortunately, we both happen to be back in tomorrow on the back shift. The last thing we need is a humongous hangover as you know. We've had a great evening and truly we are going to be sorry to see you go."

"Absolutely, don't worry about it girls. If anyone is going to understand it's me. I'm just glad that you managed to come Gina and I'll miss you too. Do your best not to overwork yourself in my absence."

The three of us say our goodbyes and they head off on their way. As I watch them walking away laughing and talking, a deep sense of realisation sets in. Wow, once they are out of my view, that will be the last time I'll ever see them, and I didn't once wish them well, for what their futures might hold. Or say to them, that I hoped everything works out. Or even to tell them to stay in touch. Yeah okay, I know that we are friends on Facebook, but come on, is that really the same as keeping in touch, let's say, over the phone? That in itself, makes me feel extremely crappy and I guess, up to a point, a little selfish too. The solution is there though, all I have to do is message them via messenger, with my contact details tomorrow and inform them that they will always be welcome to come down and visit me whenever they are free.

All the way up leading to my departure and including tonight, I've had many people come up to me to wish me luck and say that they hope that everything works out for my future. Me? All I've done is smile, nod my head, say thanks many times, and basked in the attention. Without a thought or regard to saying anything positive back to them in return. Why is human nature at times only one sided? Then once you stop and realised your own mistakes, it's too late to rectify the situation. I suppose that is something worthwhile for me to remember and work on. Generally selfish isn't a word those close to me would describe my character. I'm really giving yours truly a right self-pity party here, amazing how the alcohol can bring out many different sides to you. It's literally as though I have so many mixed personality disorders.

After I've been outside for roughly about ten minutes, I can feel my arms getting cold and goose bumps are appearing on them, so getting back up I turn to go back inside the club. Just at that exact moment where I'm about to go back in, but who shows his face none other than the gorgeous Harry, talk about good timing all we do though is stare at one another. I break the eye contact first, not able to trust myself because all my eyes seem to want to look at are his full luscious lips, wanting to feel them on mine and wanting to nibble on that bottom lip of his. So instead, I start to walk past him. As I do though, he takes hold of my hand and pulls me towards him. Man, he smells so good, just like I thought he would. His cologne does dizzying things to my senses, for a split second it feels as though my body is going to betray me. No, this cannot be allowed and damn him, he cannot do this to me. He knows what he's doing, that I'm sure of. Playing emotional flipping mind games, I've had enough of them, well no more. No man will ever play with the emotions of my heart, ever, ever, again. One minute he has tarts sprawling themselves all over him, in front of my damn face I may add. He doesn't exactly tell them to get away or to get off him. No, he is loving it, like he is getting his own personal lap dance, he was in his element. Then he thinks he can come out here to me and be a totally different kind of guy. Whose glare is so intense, so deep and filled with lust and wanting. No, I can't have this, who in the name of hell is the real Harry anyway? The guy I'm seeing in front of me now or the typical ladies' man I saw inside, who loves the ladies. Then a horrible flashback comes back to me of the way Jason and his humiliating treatment towards me and his cheating ways. All lads are the bastard same. They use women as toys or playthings, once they've had their fill and fun with us, we then get thrown to the side and discarded, as though we are worthless pieces of rubbish and they move on to the next girl without a second thought for our feelings. It's true men think with their dicks and not their brains.

Angrily, I pull myself away from Harry, he goes to grab my hand again it takes all my willpower to snatch it back from him, he looks confused and taken aback for a second.

"Go back to your leggy-blonde friend Harry, I'm sure she will be waiting in there for you."

I'm so angry with him and with myself, I do not even bother to wait for a reply. I go back inside the club to our table and find Carly and Millie with the two cute guys from earlier, obviously they have managed to make Millie cave in to their charms and I quickly make an excuse and tell them that I have a terrible onset of a headache and that I really need to get myself home. We say our goodbyes and Carly gives me a tight hug and whispers thanks into my ear for allowing her to be part of the evening celebrations. Millie kisses me on the cheek and says she'll ring me tomorrow and with that I'm out of there. So much for my last drunken farewell kiss in this city and the worst part is, I was kind of hoping that it would in fact be from Harry. I can't wait to be out of here, away from the bad memories, the poor mistakes and of course lost relationships. Fortunately, one of those relationships has started its mending process and in time mine and Carly's friendship will be strong, once more.

CHAPTER SEVENTEEN

I cannot seem to walk quickly enough, so I end up taking off my heels and start to do a gentle jog in my bare feet along the street up to the taxi rank. What a way to leave, eh? It's meant to be my leaving party and I'm the one leaving it early all because of a boy. Oh, and not forgetting the appearance that came out of nowhere, that ugly, green-eyed monster called jealousy rearing that proper unattractive head once more. I'm out of breath once I'm nearing the waiting cabs, I slow down and walk the last ten metres or thereabouts. Fortunately for me thank goodness the night is still quite young and there appears to be no queues, so I manage to get a cab straight away.

"Where to, love?"

"Pines Close, please," I reply. As we are pulling away from the curb and as we approach the traffic lights, we just manage to make it through them, just as they are turning from green to red.

I was so grateful we managed to make it through, because as we were leaving the junction where the traffic lights stand, to go left around the corner, I saw Harry sprinting up the street towards us. He appeared to have this unusual determined look to his face, one that I didn't know what to make of, actually. Well, it isn't my problem, and to be honest, with the way I'm feeling at this precise moment, I don't even give a rat's arse any more. I don't know if he noticed me in the cab and frankly, I don't really care. All that he has proven to me tonight, is that my gut instincts are right that you can't trust guys one bit, they really are as bad as each other. Once again, just like all the blokes, Harry has shown me that he can act one way to my face, but behind my back act in a totally different shitty manner and I'm not given a second thought. Yes, okay, I acknowledge and get that we are not an item or a couple I totally understand that, however what I don't understand is the logic that a guy will act in a way that he seems to be really into you and has a deep look of longing, lust and wanting in his eyes when it's just the two you, were he draws you in and all you want to do is touch his soft lips with yours — shit, talk about going of track a bit, aren't I? The least he can do though is show me some damn respect especially when we are all together in the same building and out as a group, surely. Or is that too much to ask, or am I so intoxicated with the consumption of alcohol that it's appearing that I'm proper crazy for thinking like that and making me sound completely irrational. If that is the case, then why act like you are interested in me and I know for sure that there is definitely something between us, the spark and that magnetic attraction that just oozes when we are in close proximity to one another that is incredibly overpowering, no one can possibly fake that, or can they? Was his behaviour just now, was that his way of making me jealous and to show me what I could potentially be missing when I've gone? No, in my opinion, the jerk, yes that's about right, the flipping jerk was acting immature and childish. Shit, I'm feeling so confused and the alcohol is clouding my judgement a little maybe, but how can I feel like this if I myself don't have feelings for Harry? Then out of nowhere I have a light bulb moment, no this cannot be, do I have feelings for Harry. We have been friends for so long, and yes, we have had moments in the past, granted, like Ross and Rachel in the TV sitcom *Friends*, that typical relationship that they have throughout the series. You know the one — will they, won't they, moments. We have always been flirty when we have been around each other, but I just saw that as harmless, innocent fun. Maybe these feelings have always been there, but because he was a relation of Millie's and I never wanted to jeopardise our close friendship, the mature thing was to never really act on them, and I must have buried them subconsciously, without realising it. Then I recall that moment we had over five years ago, just before Jason swept me of my feet, that was such a lost opportunity looking back now, we could have had something really good, Harry and I. With all these missed chances, that could be the universe's way of saying that we aren't meant to be, because if it was, it would have happened already.

Once safely arriving back at mine and paid the cab driver plus an extremely generous tip on top may I add. I head indoors and don't even bother to switch on any lights. As my alcohol-filled brain is fairly certain, that Harry just might make an appearance, like he did the previous night. After realising my own confusing feelings, I don't want to see him or talk to him, not tonight. My thought process in regard to acting like this is simple, I've had a bit too much to drink, I'm positively confused and not wanting to say anything or especially do anything that I may live to regret in the morning. The weaker side of my womanhood would more than likely betray me right now, seeing my missed opportunity show up on my doorstep. Knowing myself as I do, the likelihood of me jumping his bones, especially finally admitting how I deeply and truly I feel for the bloke, is incredibly likely. I must put on my sensible head so instead, I head upstairs in the complete darkness of my house, very poorly as I'm staggering around the place, get undressed, wash my make-up off my face the best I can, without being able to see properly in the dark and brush my teeth, then make my way to bed. The only thing I risk doing is reaching for my phone, I go to my iBooks and read a little until my eyelids start getting heavy and sleep comes and takes over.

I don't know how long I've been asleep for, but something stirs me from my peaceful deep slumber. I'm not even sure what it is at first that has pulled me out of my clutches of sleep. As I waken and come to, does the realisation enter my brain that it's my phone vibrating next to my head. I must have fallen asleep with it still in my hand whilst reading. I reach across and look at the screen to see who in the world would be ringing me at this ungodly hour. I groan inwardly as I see the name that has flashed up on my phone. I ignore the call completely and let it go to voicemail. What can Harry possibly have to say, that cannot wait until the morning, or at the very least at a decent bloody hour. Man, the boy can infuriate me at times. Once the ringing has stopped, I quickly go to my settings and take vibrate off, just in case he decides to call again. That way my phone will still be on silent, but I won't have it disturbing my sleep when it rings again, which I'm in no doubt and pretty sure, that it will. Once that's done, it doesn't take long before sleep takes a hold of me once more, and takes me to the land of nod.

When I do eventually wake the following morning, well for one I cannot believe the time as my eyes glance at my bedside clock — wow, it's nearly quarter past eleven. I do feel refreshed and feel far better than I should, with the ever so slightest of hangovers, that will soon pass once I've gotten something to eat and a good cup of coffee down me as well as a couple of aspirin. Secondly, I don't even bother going to check my phone as I'm not ready to face whatever may be waiting for me on there. I guarantee there'll be plenty of drunken, not-making-sense speeches from Harry, followed by lots of misspelt texts that have probably come from him too. No doubt a few from Millie too, just to check and to see if everything is okay, especially with my sudden headache attack that I used as an excuse. I do feel slightly pathetic for the way my drinking made me behave the previous evening, looking back and remembering my actions weren't the prettiest. They say that drink brings out the honesty in a person, and their true feelings. If that is the case, then surely enough for me, that is one dangerous concoction. Well for the next day and a half, no alcohol and no stupid and immature behaviour, especially when it comes to one boy in particular, until I'm far away from here.

I haven't got much in the way to eat. Well, that is a bit of an understatement actually, I have nothing in to eat as the cupboards and fridge have all been cleaned out, what with me leaving tomorrow, and tonight, I was just going to get my usual from the takeaway. So quickly I head upstairs, and get dressed and make myself somewhat respectable to be out in public. I look like a panda with my black eyes, I bloody knew I would look like this especially after washing my face in the damn darkness. See again, evidence of my immature behaviour last night. Once I look suitably decent, I get ready to go round to Pippa's. She usually gets fresh pastries in on a Saturday morning and I was wondering if she had done the same today. I grab my phone and house keys before heading out of the door. The universe however though had something else planned for me, because as soon as I open the door who appears to be sat there, as though he has been there all night, none other than Harry. Could I actually be a cow and leave him there and quietly walk by him without his knowledge? No, I couldn't possibly be that cruel to the bloke, and I did promise myself that there would be no more immature behaviour from my end. Before going to wake the sleeping beauty, I quietly slip back inside and give Pippa a quick ring and ask her, if at all possible, could she come round to mine for a little bit, and so not to worry her, I tell her the reason why. All she can do is laugh down the phone and repeat, 'Oh the poor lad'. All the while I must be sounding bitchy and peeved off at the same time. Pippa, bless her, agrees to come round, but she can only stay for about an hour or so, as she too is still incredibly busy, and has tons to do before we depart from this part of the country tomorrow. Once I hang up, my thought process goes back to Harry, and I think of the best way to handle the situation that I now unknowingly and unfairly find myself in.

Cruelly, but also incredibly funny at the same time, only one solution comes to mind and in my defence the idiot deserves it. I go to the kitchen and grab the kettle, walk to the sink and fill it up to the top with cold water, I don't bother putting the lid back on. I go back outside, stand above Harry and literally pour the whole kettle of freezing cold water over him. So much for not being immature, I simply couldn't help myself from having one last silly moment with him.

"Wakey, wakey, rise and shine, sleeping beauty."

He wakes with a splutter and a couple of explicit choice of words and all I can do is stand back laughing and watching him.

"Why the hell did you do that for? Surely there is a much better way to wake a person, Amber? Damn woman, my clothes are all wet and cold."

"Don't be so bloody soft it's only a little bit of water. How long have you been out here anyway, sitting like that? More importantly, why are you here at all, Harry? I didn't think we had anything more to say to each other."

"Well for one, we didn't actually get to say a proper goodbye to one another. Look, can I please come inside, instead of doing this on your doorstep for all your neighbours to see?"

"I still have things to do, Harry, and Pippa will be here in about ten minutes. I have to get all my packed boxes from upstairs, shifted to be down here and ready at the door as the moving van will be here in a few hours. I simply don't have the time to deal with this Harry. Please just say what you need to say and let's not make this any more awkward than it has to be, okay?"

Neither of us moves or talks for a minute or two, then I see Harry giving his head the slightest of nods and then he prances to his feet and walks over to me. Before I can do anything, he puts his hands on either side of my face in the most gentle and loving way, he gives his lips the smallest of licks to moisten them. Then before I have time to prepare myself for what's about to happen his lips are pressed against

167

mine, he's kissing me in such a tender way and I'm responding in such a hunger that I take myself by surprise. I feel his tongue parting my lips and starting to brush against my own tongue. Wow, we've kissed before, but this is different, I feel the intensity of it throughout my body, filled with such warmth and promise, and do I dare to say it? — love. My womanly parts are awakening and betraying me at the same time. I want more, but in the same breath knowing that isn't possible I'm leaving tomorrow and there is no way that I'm willing to stay, not even for Harry and I wouldn't ask him to leave his life up here and move with me. That wouldn't be fair to him and I don't think I could cope with the guilt of him making that decision, especially if it didn't work out between the two of us. No, a clean break, with hundreds of miles to separate us, only then will we know if those feelings we share are genuine, and if they are, then who knows? No one truly knows what the future holds, well apart from God, obviously, and he won't tell us.

I pull back abruptly before anything else can happen and plus I think we are giving my neighbours a show that they don't need to see. Harry rests his forehead against mine and closes his eyes.

"Is there any chance of you staying, Amber, any chance at all?"

I step back from him with tears in my eyes, thinking how once again the timing is all wrong, the universe is really wanting to keep us parted. Nevertheless, and as much as this may hurt, I look at him directly, so he knows I mean what I'm about to say, without trying to be mean or cruel. I just want to be honest with him.

"I'm so sorry, Harry, but I'm done with this place. I'm ready to start my new life in a whole new place. I really don't want to stay. I'm looking forward to this new chapter I am about to start. Once again, we seem to find ourselves in this situation, where it is just completely and utterly the wrong timing for us, maybe the universe is trying to say that we are just not meant to be, we are just meant to be really good friends. Saying that though, I would be lying if I didn't want it to happen because if things were different, I do believe we would be great together. Unfortunately, now isn't our time, maybe in another life."

Harry for the first time that I've known him has tears streaming down his face. All he does is give me a watery smile, takes hold of my face once more and gently presses a warm, wet tender kiss to my lips.

"Goodbye, Amber."

With that he walks away from me, out of my life and doesn't look back, not once. Whereas here, I'm left on my doorstep, hugging myself tightly as though my life depended on it, crying as though my heart is breaking once more. I don't take my eyes off him until he is completely out of view. I know I could have asked him to come with me but there was something stopping me and that was fear of getting hurt. I don't think I could go through that again. With Harry, if the worst happened my pain and heartbreak would be ten times worse than it ever was with Jason. Because I do believe that Harry is the one for me, in every sense of the word. With that discovery I finally realise that I love him. I'm in love with Harry, and that my heart belongs to him, and maybe, it always has, and always will do.

CHAPTER EIGHTEEN

Wow I cannot believe it, the day has finally arrived. I'm here actually standing on the platform at the train station waiting for the train to arrive with Pippa and our suitcases. We thought that we would pack a case each and carry it with us, just with some spare underwear, change of clothing and obviously the most important is to have our toiletries to hand. Like Pippa said yesterday, we don't want to be rummaging through boxes after the long journey we are about to do. Be best to pack a couple of days' clothing, and Pippa, who has done this trip countless times, will know best. Millie and surprisingly Carly, have both come to wave us off, my reason for being so surprised at Carly, is she is never one to rise before midday, not for anyone or anything, or she could have been up all night, partying, and came straight here instead of going home. That's the cynical part of my brain working and I feel guilty for thinking that way, it is hard not to though when it comes to Carly. Well, whatever the case I'm really glad that she's made the effort and came though and I'm happy that we have, in some kind of way, sorted some things out and moved on.

Well, here we are the four of us, on a dark, cloudy and gloomy day which actually suits the sadness that is hanging around us. The atmosphere feels heavy as though something is about to happen, which is stupid I know. Obviously, Harry is a no show, but really that doesn't surprise me one iota, not after yesterday to be fair to him. However, I don't know if I'm happy or not with his absence, to be fair though I don't think I could handle seeing him cry once again, that was an awful sight to witness yesterday and knowing that I was the cause of it didn't bode well for me. I feel that image will stay with me for quite a while, if truth be told. I suppose there really isn't much left to say between the two of us and if he was here all there would be is a lot of uncomfortable small talk to fill the awkward silence. No, we had the perfect goodbye yesterday, it was personal and private unless he has mentioned any of it to Millie, but she hasn't dropped any hints that he has. In a way, that last kiss we shared, said so much, and in the same sense, didn't say enough.

"I just need to quickly pop to the ladies, I'll shalt be a minute."

"Don't be too long pet, the train will be here shortly."

I leave the three of them talking amongst themselves and promise Pippa I will only be a couple of minutes.

I needed to make an excuse to pardon myself from the girls, as I needed a moment alone to be with my thoughts and also to get under control the burning sensation I can feel on the backs of my eyes, as the tears are building up. Once I've finished having some time alone, and got myself composed and on my way back to the girls, I notice myself checking the time and looking around me searching for that one person I want to see the most, just to see if I can catch a glimpse of Harry. Part of me hoping, that he may have changed his mind and actually came to say goodbye, one last time, not just to me but Pippa as well. Maybe that is a bit of wishful thinking on my part, but a girl can hope, can't she? Yesterday morning, has been preying on my mind over and over again and having a massive effect on my thought process. Second guessing myself, wondering if I handled the whole situation right, or did I say things that didn't necessarily needed to be even mentioned, or even just say something that was never talked about. What was done is done and what was said, well, there really wasn't anything left to say, was there? No regrets now Amber, time to move forward and leave the past where it belongs, it's all part of your own personal history. I say to myself, as a form of a pep talk.

You see, that's the thing when it comes to me and Harry, I don't think we have ever once sat down just the two of us and had a deep meaningful conversation just about us and what could potentially be there, simmering away at the service between ourselves. Yes, we flirt a lot and we can have a laugh and joke around, of course there has been a few occasions where we have shared a few kisses here and there over the years and recently there has been some quite intimate and tender moments. Never once though have we thought to sit down together and discuss what it might mean. Well, minus Harry's efforts yesterday morning, bless him. We truly are as bad as each other in every sense of the word, because I could have initiated a conversation, but instead, just like Harry, I too have avoided it and acted as though it was all nothing, just some innocent fooling around. Well, in my case, I think deep down, I'm still hurting incredibly badly after Jason, and that kind of pain and betrayal can stick with you for some time, where your barriers and walls will hardly ever come down, for fear of being hurt once more. Now though, well now it's too late. All

I can hope for is that time and the distance between Harry and I can mend our friendship at the very least.

As I arrive back to the platform and stand with the girls my phone goes and makes a ping sound indicating I have a message. It makes me chuckle, because speak of the devil, as though he knew I was just thinking of him and he could sense he was on my mind, Harry has sent me a message. I don't want to read it in front of everyone, so without drawing too much attention to who it is, I simply put my phone away and wait till I'm safely on the train before having the strength to read it.

"Have you got everything that you need for the journey, love?" Pippa asks me.

"Of course, you're talking to a travelling expert, don't you know," I jokily respond.

Just then, we notice the train in the distance, making its way slowly towards the station. We all hurriedly give each other hugs, and I tell the girls I'll text them once we've arrived safely. I give Carly a tight hug and whisper in her ear, that all was forgiven and that I loved her and will miss her. I quickly tell her how glad I am that we have patched things up. Then I go and hug Millie and I start crying.

"What you bleeding crying for, you sloppy cow, you'll be seeing me next month, and possibly have me as a permanent room-mate."

"I'm still going to miss you in the meantime, I love you Mils."

"I love you too Amber, I'll be down there before you know it."

Me and Pippa grab our suitcases and with the help of one of

the train staff, who helps us with our luggage onto the train, I let Pippa get on first. I turn to give my friends one last wave then turn and go to follow Pippa into our carriage to find our seats. Within a minute or two the train gives its signal and we are slowly pulling away from the station platform and we are finally on our way.

"You okay, Pet?"

"I'm all good, thanks for asking, Pippa."

"Any regrets?"

I look towards the woman who has been there for me, my surrogate mother and I smile to her.

"No Pippa. no regrets, none at all."

As I sit back in my seat and look out of the window, I smile to myself, knowing that deep down, that is the truth. I simply have no regrets. I then reach for my phone and read Harry's message:

Hi, Amber, it would have been far too painful for me to watch you leave on that train. To me, I think we had the perfect goodbye yesterday, don't you think so too. Send a quick text when you get there. Safe travels, take care. LOVE H xxx

It puts a smile on my face and it doesn't escape my notice that for the first time ever he has signed off his message with *Love*. My thoughts quickly go to, is this his way of saying that he loves me? Or am I looking for signs that simply aren't there?

I quickly send him one back:

> Hi Harry, I suppose we did
> have the perfect goodbye, didn't
> we. Yes, that is me agreeing
> with you for once haha. You
> take care of yourself, you
> hear me and stay in touch.
> Love A XXX

I think that's the first time I've actually put the word love into one of my texts to him. Okay, yes, I know, it's not me telling him, Harry, I love you, but it's close enough, and what's the point of me telling him now anyway. I put my phone away, and get my book that I brought just for the journey, before I know it though, with all the pent-up emotions of the last forty-eight hours, I have drifted off to the land of nod.

CHAPTER NINETEEN

I am so tired after nearly six hours on the train and two changes, one at Crewe and the second one at Wolverhampton. Pippa and I have finally arrived into Southampton Central train station. It is nearing five o'clock so I'm hoping we manage to get a cab as it is just before the start of rush hour and quite a few people got off the train with us. I am hungry and in need of a much-needed strong cup of coffee. I could also do with doing some yoga stretches to iron out some of the knots in my lower back, as it is a little sore, and feeling quite stiff, from sitting for such a long time.

"This way, Pet," Pippa says to me.

I grab my suitcase and follow Pippa along the platform, until we reach some stairs that we need to go up and cross the bridge to get to the other side and through the ticket barriers to get outside. As we approach the barriers however, I do a double take, because out of nowhere, I see Sandy from the TV show on Channel four, called *Gogglebox*. Obviously, I ask her for a selfie but wasn't possible, as she refused, because apparently her agent has said she needs to charge people for one. So instead, I wish her well and say my goodbyes, and Pippa and I make our way outside.

Straight away I notice the massive difference in the temperature. The sun is really blazing and there isn't a cloud to been seen for miles. I tilt my head backwards so my face is up towards the heavenly skies and just take in the glorious heat. I can actually feel it seeping into my pale skin, wow, I could literally bake in this sunshine. Pippa wasn't wrong was she, when she said it was quite a few degrees warmer down south. Honestly, I thought that she was slightly over exaggerating. It is so blissful. Oh, I could definitely get used to this, that's for sure. Apparently, I've read somewhere on the internet when I was googling information about the Isle of Wight, that it gets five hundred more hours of sunshine, than the rest of the UK. If that's true, then I'm in for some good weather and beach days.

"Come on, love, there are a few taxis left, this way now."

"I'm coming, Pippa, I was just soaking up some of this heat. How long do you reckon it will be before we manage to get to the Island?"

"Depends on the ferry love to be honest, hopefully it is running on time and isn't delayed for whatever reason. Also depends on how many people are waiting to get on it, if it is full to capacity then we will have to wait for the next one. Once we are in the taxi then it will only take no more than ten minutes or so, we should be able to catch the seventeen thirty-five ferry, to Cowes, and Pebble Bank Bay."

We manage to get the last waiting taxi and I can't help looking out of my window at all the new surroundings all around me. I do feel like a child, I've got that typical goofy grin on my face, excitement at all the new wonders of a new, magical place.

Once we have passed Southampton town centre, the sudden smell of the salt from the sea fills the air and I know that we are getting close to the harbour and my stomach gets that typical butterfly sensation feeling, you know when you are extremely excited about something. Man, what is wrong with me? I'm a grown-arse woman, for crying out loud, not an over-bearing, excitable toddler. However, my joyous mood becomes a little deflated when we arrive at the ferry terminal. Once we have paid the taxi driver and got our suitcases, we slowly approach the gangway and I am shocked with the queue forming already, luckily for us there is only about forty people standing in line before us, give or take a few. Then a thought occurs to me that we may not be able to actually board this one. Shit, I think to myself, I am already aching everywhere, my feet are killing, my back is really playing up, all I want is for this journey to be over with now. I could really do with an all-over body massage, and to sleep for twenty-four hours, without waking up. It makes me wonder how Pippa does this, time and time again.

"How many people can they fit onto one of these Pippa, do you think we will have to stand?" I hope and pray that we don't.

"No one is allowed to stand up on this ferry, Amber, everyone has to sit in the seats and belt themselves in. They even give you an on-board safety guide, like they do when you fly in a plane."

"Oh okay, so how many can they actually fit onto one of these then?"

"Em, I would say somewhere between two hundred and fifty, and maybe two hundred and eighty. Something like that. They are surprisingly big on the inside, far bigger than they look like from the outside."

"Awesome, then we should definitely be able to get onto

this next one then."

"Yes, why love, are you starting to get tired now?"

"Well, I won't lie, Pippa, but that last surge of energy was taken with my overexcitement at looking at all my new surroundings, to be honest. I am though starting to feel a bit of fatigue coming on."

It does make me wonder not for the first time how Pippa did this trip at least three times a year every year for who knows how long? Especially at her age. You could go on a long-haul flight to a lovely Caribbean destination, with the hours we have put in so far to get here.

"I'm starting to feel a bit weary myself too. At least I won't need to do this journey ever again, and hopefully that's the same for you too, Amber."

I know that Pippa is desperate for me to like it down here and I know that she will do everything in her power to make sure that happens, and if truth be told, secretly so am I. I'm already liking what I'm seeing so far.

It's weird because as I'm stood here waiting in line, there all around me is nothing but the Southern accent and it makes me break out into a smile. There is no Northern dialect to be heard at all. It really is like that famous line out of the classic movie *The Wizard of Oz*, well, Amber you're not in Kansas any more. Well, in truth, you're not in Cumbria, any more. The ferry has now come into port, it is so funning watching the people coming off and all rushing to get to their taxis or the bus, that will be waiting for them. It really is like watching a group of normal people sprinting the one hundred metres, in this case though you have parents grabbing hold of their children's hands and literally pulling them along and the little legs and feet of the kids practically being dragged across the floor. The older generation who cannot run are doing their best to speed walk in some kind of way, so that they can get from A to B as fast as is humanly possible for them. Once we have finally embarked the ferry, me and Pippa manage to get a couple of seats near the window after safely putting our suitcases in the luggage area, making sure that they won't move or roll. Finally, once the ferry has reached its capacity, and the doors are closed, I look out of my window and I've a surreal feeling that goes through me. I cannot really explain it, either. Whilst I watch us pulling away from port, it feels like I'm leaving my country behind and moving to a whole new one. It is such an unreal feeling knowing that I won't or don't in fact from now on live on mainland England, I'm not too sure how to really feel about that. Will life really be that much different? Whatever they don't have on the island, will I have to keep coming back and forth on the ferry? If that is the case, then it's going to be quite expensive. I guess that was one thing that wasn't taken into the equation and I hadn't weighed up properly when I was thinking this through. Well I guess what will be, will be and for now I'm going to enjoy the ride and see what comes at the end of it.

We could have got the car ferry, where we would have gone on as foot passengers. That though takes a lot longer to cross the Solent. Roughly around an hour and fifteen minutes, whereas the one we are on now only takes about twenty-five minutes, because it is smaller and faster and only takes foot passengers. I am pleasantly surprised at the smoothness of the journey, it literally feels like we are gliding across the tops of the water. Saying that though the sea is quite calm today, not that I suffer from sea sickness or anything because I don't. I simply hate being bounced around, it's like when you fly and you hit air turbulence and the plane rattles and shakes a little, no one likes that either. Well, it's the same kind of thing on the water.

It isn't long before I start to see the outline of the Isle of Wight and as we get closer the first thing that my eagle eyes notice is the long pebble beach, which I now know is called Pebble Bank Bay, and from what I can make out from this distance, are people sunbathing on their towels. You can see children and adults out in the water having fun and swimming. Wow, what a lifestyle these people have, well the ones that live here. I also notice all the different shapes and sizes of the sailing boats, out in the open waters. It really is like I am witnessing a whole new world here. The water is an amazing shade of colours from deep green to blue, then turquoise. The way the rays of the sun is hitting the water, like glistening magical fairy dust floating and gently bobbing around with the waves. It is just breathtakingly beautiful and this is going to be my home, it just feels so surreal that I have to pinch myself to make sure this is not a dream.

"We are coming into the terminal now Amber."

"Wow, it is just beautiful, Pippa. I don't know what I was expecting, but it sure wasn't beauty like this."

"Wait until you see the small town, it really is like you have been transported to a French town in a way, that's where its former name, Shamblord, comes from."

"I thought that the name sounded French… Shamblord."

"Well as you get to know the island more, you'll notice that a lot of the towns and small villages have French names.

The French at one point, many, many, years ago, invaded the island. William the Conquer resided here, before the battle of Hastings in ten sixty-six."

"Wow, it sounds like the island is steeped in history, I will have to do some research and find out more. So does Dawn actually live here and work here in Cowes then, Pippa?"

"Yes, she could never leave this place, she loves it too much. As do I if truth be told. It really does feel like you are in a whole new world and the lifestyle is so relaxed and chilled, with a much slower pace. Dawn's business, The Beach Cove Cafe, isn't exactly here in the town. It's at the other side of Pebble Bank Bay, about two and a half miles away."

Once the ferry has docked, we are then allowed to remove our seat belts and get up, so we go and retrieve our suitcases and make our way to disembark. Once again it is a mad frenzy, people trying to get out of the terminal as quick as they possibly can. I just give my head a little shake and chuckle to myself.

Once we have managed to get out of the terminal ourselves, I'm taken by surprise to discover that we have come out in the town of Cowes, right next to the marina. Straight away the salt from the sea hits my nostrils and I can taste the sea salt in the air, small particles which have landed onto my lips and I take in a deep breath and enjoy the scent in the air, whilst I follow behind Pippa. The first thing that I notice is the cute little nail bar that's called Polished Finished, which I know for sure that at some point I will definitely be booking an appointment in the not too distant, future. Next door to that is a lovely little cafe called Sweet and Savoury Delights, with cute little tables and chairs outside the front of it. It looks like they do every kind of pancakes and crêpes from different sweet fillings all the way to savoury delights. Mmmm, very French, I think to myself. I will have to for sure have to try one of their savoury crêpes. The smells that are coming from there, when we pass it, is mouth-wateringly delicious, and makes my stomach rumble.

Once we leave the port, I find myself in the heart of the cute little town that will now be my home. It is the cutest of towns that my eyes have ever seen in a really long time and I totally understand and get where Pippa is coming from. It really does feel like a typical Mediterranean holiday town, especially with all the hustle and bustle and that holiday smell in the air. People are sitting outside cafes drinking coffee and having a smoke with their mates, laughing and chatting. Others are outside pubs and adorable little wine bars. You have the prettiest homemade ice-cream parlours. Designer clothes stores, yachting and boating stores with paddle boards in the windows on display, butchers, home-grown fruit and veg stores, bakeries and patisseries shops, fishmongers with freshly daily-caught fish. All self-owned businesses, it really does feel like I have stepped into another world, a world that I'm really not used to at all. None of your typical Greggs bakeries, or Subway sandwich shops anywhere. Everything looks to be island-produced. The architecture is breath-taking in certain parts of the town, you can tell it has had European influences and is really old. It's just simply put, absolutely splendid and already I love it and could very much fall in love with this place, now seeing it for myself and completely and utterly understanding now why Dawn could never leave this place. Boy, Pippa must have found it extremely difficult to leave this marvellous place, every time she had to say goodbye. There is a woman approaching us, and she looks the double of Pippa, just a few years older, and her smile widens on her face as she stops in front of us. This must be Dawn, she pulls Pippa close to her bosom and hugs her tightly.

"I'm over the moon to finally see you here for good this time, knowing I'll never have to wave goodbye to you again." The warm tenderness of her affection is so overwhelming, that I feel my eyes mist over.

"Dawn let me introduce you to Amber, Amber this is my sister Dawn." I smile my hello and just like she did with Pippa, Dawn grabs hold of me and hugs my so tightly that I think she might break a rib.

"Lovely to meet you at long last, dear child. I've heard so much about you. Pippa says you're the daughter she never had, so I guess you'll be my niece, by default," she cheekily winks to me.

Following this startling revelation, Dawn then grabs my face between her hands and kisses me on each cheek, I already like the woman very much and I know we will get on like a house on fire. Suddenly a warm unexpected feeling washes over me as I look around my current surroundings and make a start to walk towards the cafe along the beach front. It's as though an inner spirit is talking to me, and somehow, I know that I'm where I'm supposed to be, and I've finally come home.

To
Be
Continued…